HOT
LIKE FIRE

D0182088

NIOBIA
BRYANT

Kensington Publishing Corp.

http://www.kensingtonbooks.com

DAFINA BOOKS are published by

Kensington Publishing Corp.
850 Third Avenue
New York, NY 10022

Copyright © 2007 by Niobia Bryant

All Kensington Titles, Imprints, and Distributed Lines are available at special quantity discounts for bulk purchases for sales
promotions, premiums, fund-raising, and educational or insti-
tutional use. Special book excerpts or customized printings can
also be created to fit specific needs. For details, write or phone
the office of the Kensington special sales manager: Kensington
Publishing Corp., 850 Third Avenue, New York, NY 10022,
attn: Special Sales Department, Phone: 1-800-221-2647.

Dafina and the Dafina logo Reg. U.S. Pat. & TM Off.

ISBN-13: 978-0-7582-1461-4
ISBN-10: 0-7582-1461-8

First mass market printing: November 2007

10 9 8 7 6 5 4 3 2 1

Printed in the United States of America

Reviews of Previous Niobia Bryant Books

Also by
NIOBIA BRYANT

Romance

Admission of Love * +
Three Times a Lady
Heavenly Match * +
Can't Get Next To You <>
Let's Do It Again
Count on This <>
Heated + §
Hot Like Fire + §

Women's Fiction

Live and Learn
Show and Tell

Anthologies

Could it Be? in *You Never Know*

KEY

* Connected Books
+ Books set in Holtsville, SC (Hot Holtsville Series)
<> Connected Books (The Dutton Sisters Series)
§ Connected Books (The Strong Family Series)

For my grandparents
Sally and Clarence Johnson

I bet they're kissing in heaven.

Prologue

"¿Me das este baile?"

Garcelle Santos looked over her bare shoulder at the tall and handsome dark-skinned man requesting a dance at the wedding reception of Kahron Strong and his new bride, Bianca. The man was Bianca Strong's friend from Atlanta. Armand Touissant.

There was no denying the interest in his eyes, but Garcelle was looking for nothing more than someone to dance and maybe laugh with. She smiled as she placed her hand in his and let him twirl her rather dramatically onto the center of the dance floor. She actually flung her head back and laughed as he pulled her body to his while Syleena Johnson's "I Am Your Woman" played.

"You are one of the most beautiful women I've ever seen in my life," he whispered in her ear, with his hand at the small of her back.

"Thank you," was all that Garcelle said. She hoped that was the end of the talking.

But he continued with his compliments, even trying to press Garcelle's body closer to his. She stepped back from him, with a chastising smile. As

8 *Niobia Bryant*

they two-stepped, she looked over his broad shoulder with her beautiful, doe-shaped eyes. All of Holtsville was in attendance. Some faces she recognized, and others she didn't.

Kahron and Bianca were dancing together in a playful and sexy way. There was no denying the love and passion. *The fire burns between them so strongly,* Garcelle thought, wishing them well as Armand guided their bodies into a series of turns.

Bianca's father, Hank, was dancing with that whacky Mimi. They made an odd pair: he was so tall and broad, while she was so petite and crazy as hell. Garcelle just shook her head at that pairing.

Kaeden and Kaleb, two of Kahron's brothers, stood at the bar watching a pretty, dark-skinned beauty saunter by. Kaleb said something, and both men looked absolutely wolfish before they laughed. The Strong men really were strikingly handsome, particularly when all four of the brothers were together. Somehow each of them made having prematurely grey hair the sexiest thing ever.

But one was missing. The mean and sullen one.

Feeling mischievous, Garcelle swung her head to the left and then to the right. *How like him not to enjoy the festivities.* When Armand again sent their bodies into a series of turns that drew the attention of the crowd, Garcelle caught a glimpse of silver curls and broad shoulders over in the rear of the reception tent. *Alone.* She whipped her head around and looked at him, only to find that his intense stare was already locked on her. Her heart raced madly.

He had once angered her when he accused her of stealing. That day they had insulted each other like children, and now they barely spoke to one another. But she couldn't deny that of all the sexy

Strong brothers, he was the most divine. And the thought of his eyes on her made her *muy caliente.*

The music changed to an up-tempo song, and Garcelle broke free of Armand's hold, grabbed the full skirts of her crimson dress, and began dancing the salsa all alone. Soon the dance floor cleared, and she was left alone to give in to the passion and electricity of the dance. But she noticed no one. No one but Kade.

Her eyes were locked on him. Even when she spun, she would stop so that she was facing him, and their eyes would lock once more. With each of her spins, she found he was moving closer and closer to the edge of the dance floor.

Garcelle enjoyed the warmth of his eyes as she handled the footwork with ease. The crowd applauded her. She moved her body like a snake when need be. She gyrated her hips like she was working a hoola hoop. She danced like her life was dependent on it.

She danced for him, and even though he stood there, with his hands in his pants pocket, his face the same brooding and unchanging mask, she knew he had not missed one bit of it.

When the music came to an end, Garcelle spun her body across the dance floor until she came to a dramatic stop before him, with her flared skirt floating in the air before it slowly drifted down around her shapely legs. Everyone applauded her, but Garcelle's eyes were locked on Kade's. Pure electricity ran through her body.

Even as she moved away from him, casting one last look at him over her shoulder, Garcelle knew that in that one moment, *everything* between them had changed.

1

Two Months Later

As soon as the alarm clock sounded and woke him from his sleep, Kade Strong rolled out of bed. No snoozing. No lounging. No adjusting to being awake. No sitting on the side of the bed until he got out of that half asleep–half awake zone. Just up and at 'em. It was time for a hard day's work, and he didn't mind it one bit.

Five years ago, when his father decided to semi-retire from running the daily operation of the ranch, he turned it over to Kade, his oldest son. And Kade had been profoundly touched that his father had entrusted him with Strong Ranch. Kade had always worked the ranch along with his brothers, but now he initiated new ideas and made it his business to take the ranch into the future. So he went from paid manager of the farm to part owner. He never wanted to fail his father or ruin a highly successful business. So if continued success meant working right along with their forty ranch hands from dawn to dusk, then Kade was more than willing to do it. Besides, he always had been a hands-on type of man. Sitting in an office, making sure he didn't get dirt under his nails, wasn't his thing.

Nude, he strode into the adjoining bath of his bedroom and relieved himself, with a long sigh. After flushing the commode, he stretched before he started the shower. He looked down at the sink. One washcloth. One towel. One toothbrush. One rinse cup. One of everything in his life. Constant reminders that he was alone now.

It had been close to three years since his wife, Reema, had passed away. Years that seemed like forever without her.

That's why he hated to be in bed alone. A pillow to hold at night was a poor substitute for spooning his wife. Holding her. Smelling the scent of her hair and her neck. Teasing her nipples in the last moments before he dozed off. Her hand reaching back to lightly rest on his thigh. Their innocent embrace suddenly turning to hot caresses and the most passionate lovemaking ever. The unique scent of their sex. Intimacy. Affection. Love.

Sighing, he stepped inside the shower, pulling the curtain closed as the steam surrounded his body. As he began to lather his washcloth, his elbow slammed against the tiled wall. He winced and swore. The dimensions of the bathtub left a lot to be desired for a man of his size. Six foot five and 225 pounds, Kade was solid and strong. Trying to shower—or God help him—bathe in a bathroom fit for someone under six feet was more injurious to his body than working the ranch.

For a second, as he dragged the soapy cloth across his ridged abdomen, he thought of the master suite at his own house. Reema had made sure everything had been custom built to fit him. The high ceilings. The extra long bed. The oversized Jacuzzi tub. The tiled shower big enough for him to spin in.

The night before Reema died had been his last night in that house. He hadn't been back since. He hadn't wanted to return.

Kade finished his shower and rushed to get dressed in one of the nearly thirty Dickies uniforms in the closet. As soon as he pulled on his Tims, he left the room and walked across the hall to look in on his seven-year-old daughter, Kadina. Even though he knew she was sleeping, because of the predawn hour, every workday he liked to look in on her before he went out to work the ranch.

She was the only thing that had kept him sane in the first few months after Reema's death. He had had to at least pretend to be strong for his child. Strong. Humph, sometimes he had found it so hard to live up to his name.

Kade shut her bedroom door and jogged down the stairs. The scent of coffee hit him before he even reached the bottom step. Ever since he was a little boy, his mother had gotten up with his father, made him a cup of coffee, and fixed his breakfast before he left to work the ranch every day. Thirty years later, the tradition lived on.

At the sight of his parents, Kade came to a halt just before stepping into the kitchen. His father, Kael, was sliding his hand under his mother's knee-length gown. It was not exactly the warm family scene Kade wanted to be a part of.

Kade backtracked and headed down the hall to the front door. As badly as he craved his morning cup of coffee, he wanted to respect his parent's privacy. He lived with them, and he didn't want to be an intrusion.

Kade jogged down the stairs and climbed into his Ford Expedition. Although he had every intention of heading toward the rear of the ranch, he followed an instinct and, instead, steered his vehicle down the winding road leading to the main highway, in the direction of Summerville, South Carolina. His heart raced a bit as he eventually made the turn off of Highway 17. His grip on the wheel tightened. His body jostled as he drove down the dirt road, swerving around crater-sized potholes.

Set back in the center of three acres of land was *the* house. His house. He climbed out of the SUV, with his eyes fixed on the two-level brick structure of over three thousand square feet. With the Strong Ranch hands keeping up the maintenance of the land as he requested, it appeared to be a warm home awaiting the return of the family, but that house had not been a home for years.

Kade slid his large hands into the pockets of his navy Dickies pants. The silver curls of his prematurely gray hair glistened in the rising sun. Memories unfolded before him like a movie, causing a soft smile to play at his supple lips.

Kade climbed the steps, with his keys in hand, but the front door swung open before he reached the top step. He was surrounded by the sweet and subtle scent of his wife's perfume just before she leaned her tall, full, and curvaceous figure against the door frame, with a welcoming smile filled with the love he knew she had for him.

He paused for a second at the top step as his love—that deep, lasting, one-of-a-kind love—filled his chest. Reema was his wife, his friend, his lover, the mother of his child, the keeper of his secrets, and the believer in his dreams. He couldn't imagine his life without her.

"Hey, you," he greeted her as his smile broadened and his bottomless dimples deepened. It was their first night in their new home. The first of many more to come.

Reema flung her braids over her shoulders as she stepped forward to press her hands against his broad chest and her lips to his. "Welcome home, baby," she said softly against his mouth.

Their eyes locked as Kade pressed his hands against her hips and deepened the kiss.

"Kadina's upstairs napping. Dinner's in the oven keeping warm. . . ."

Kade grinned wolfishly as he bent slightly to swing her ample, curvaceous body up into his strong arms with well-practiced ease. He stepped inside the house and used his foot to kick the front door closed behind them.

The image faded, and Kade swallowed a lump in his throat. He literally shook away the sadness as a tear raced down his cheek. He released a heavy breath and wiped his face.

He leaned back against the SUV and looked up. Everything was calm and serene. He used to love this time of the day. Every morning, before he left their home, Reema would rise with him, just like his mother did for his father. She would fix breakfast, and they would sit on the patio outside the kitchen and watch the sun rise.

It had been so long since he'd let himself enjoy something so simple yet so beautiful. He missed this. He missed a lot of things. His wife. His home. His bed. His privacy. His life.

* * *

Kahron Strong sped up Highway 17, heading back from Charleston. He had just made a run to Lowe's for supplies and was anxious to get back to his ranch. Cattle that he purchased at the livestock auction last week were being delivered today, and he was anxious not to miss it. His masculine hands drummed the steering wheel as he listened to "Don't Matter" by Akon, playing on his satellite radio. He was singing along off-key as he looked out at the stretches of emerald green trees and grass lining the highway.

He smiled as he thought of his wife, Bianca. She was a tall, fair-skinned beauty with luscious lips he could suckle forever. She was everything he never knew he wanted. *Everything.*

The wide screen of his BlackBerry lit up where it sat on the passenger seat of his truck. He quickly turned down the volume of the radio and reached for it. His heart skipped a beat.

"Hey, you," he said, his voice filled with warmth, pleasure, and love.

"Hey, you," Bianca said in return, her voice husky with sleep and emotion. "I wanted to see you before you left the house this morning."

"I didn't want to wake you, since you got in so late last night," he said, placing his signature rimless aviator shades atop his silver faded head as he steered the vehicle easily with one hand.

"And *because* I came in so late, I had something I wanted to *give you* this morning."

Kahron's smile broadened at the obvious sexy intent in his wife's voice. He loved and adored the woman. His woman.

When he first saw Bianca King driving her flashy convertible as her riot of curls blew in the wind, he never imagined the mysterious woman would later become the love of his life. She was the one person that knew him better than anyone else.

His eyes shifted to the digital clock on the dash. "I'll be home in ten minutes."

"I'll be waiting."

Kahron felt anticipation fill him as he ended the call and propelled the vehicle forward. Bianca was not only an equine veterinarian servicing the local farms in the area, but also co-owner and operator of King Equine Services, and her time had been stretched thin lately. They had to make time for each other. Since they were used to making love once daily—if not more—they had some making up to do for the last few weeks of their marriage.

Kahron's head swung toward Kade's house as he passed it. He did a double take before quickly pulling his SUV off the paved road and slamming on his brakes. Dirt and pebbles flew up around him. Quickly, he checked for traffic in his mirror before he did an illegal U-turn. He squinted his eyes as he turned left onto the unpaved road leading to Kade's home.

His heart literally ached to see his older brother obviously struggling to enter the house. It was well known that Kade had not been at the house since the night before his wife passed. Kahron wanted to go to him, help him through such an obvious big step in his life, but another part of him knew Kade wanted to do it alone.

Kahron released a heavy and expectant breath as his brother's tall frame finally disappeared through the front door. He snatched up his BlackBerry and quickly dialed the number even as he climbed out of the SUV. "Hey, I need everyone to get over to Kade's ASAP."

Kade was lost in memories he had pushed away and protected from his grief. As he drifted slowly through the house, each room shook some buried emotion from him. Each brought some seemingly insignificant moment in time to the forefront.

He paused in each room as his life played out before him like a movie. Late nights in the den, cuddled with Reema on the couch, watching movies. Coming home late from work and sitting in the nursery to just hold Kadina as she slept. Waking up every morning to that poster-sized photo of them smiling on their wedding day.

His emotions ran the gamut and left him shaky.

In his bedroom, Kade sunk down at the foot of the bed and looked up at the photo as he locked his fingers between his knees. He felt spent. He felt weak. Drained. Depleted. Lost. Incomplete. But for the first time in years, he also felt hope, peace, and confidence that he was ready for the future. As one lone tear raced down his cheek, he stood and walked out of the house, knowing it was time to move on with life.

Kade paused as he stepped out onto the porch. Surprise filled his handsome face, and he quickly wiped the moisture from high cheekbones. His deep-set eyes took in each compassion-filled face of his family as they stood at the base of the steps. His parents, Kael and Lisha Strong. Kaleb, Kaeden, Kaitlyn, and Kahron and Bianca. Somehow he wasn't at all surprised to see them there. Not at all.

"You okay, son?" Kael called out in that deep baritone voice of his as he hugged his wife close to his side.

Kade nodded as he descended the few steps into their midst. "I'm good. In fact, I'm better than I've been in a long time."

Kaitlyn stepped forward and wrapped her arm around his waist. "What's going on?" she asked, bumping her hip against his side.

He lifted his hand to muss her short crop of dyed jet-black hair. "I've decided that Kadina and I are going to move back into the house," he told them, playfully looking down at his palm for dye before he wiped his hand on his pants leg. The brothers all loved teasing their baby sister about dyeing the grey out of her hair.

Kaitlyn just gave him a saucy eye roll.

Even as his brothers all stepped forward to either hug him close or clap him soundly on the back, and his sister and sister-in-law kissed his cheek, he saw the immediate concern on his mother's face. Kade moved through the small group and pulled her into a tight embrace.

He smiled at the way her head barely reached his chest. "We'll be fine, Ma," he assured her as she squeezed him tightly.

"Did we say or do something?" she asked, tilting her head back to look up at him. "You know how much I love having Kadina and you around the house."

"It's just time. That's all," replied Kade. "That's the *only* reason."

Her eyes searched his for a few moments before she hugged him one last time and nodded her head in understanding. Then she stepped back from him.

Kaeden stepped forward to playfully punch Kade's

arm. "My big brother just wants to get back to normal, right?"

Kade nodded. "Right," he agreed. "Now I want to say . . . especially while you're all here," Kade continued, giving each of his brothers a long and meaningful stare. "I'm not ready for this to become a bachelor pad, with women coming in and out of here quicker than cars at a drive-thru window."

Each of the brothers nodded in understanding, and Kade hoped they truly did understand. His eyes took in that comfortable and loving way Bianca massaged his brother's back, and he glanced away. He hated to admit to the jealousy he felt about their intimacy.

"Well, who's gonna help you with Kadina?" Lisha asked. "Getting her ready for school when you're already up and at the ranch. Her hair. Her meals."

Bianca pulled a rubber band from the back pocket of her jeans and gathered her hair into a ponytail. "I agree, Kade. You're going to need help. So much of your time is wrapped up in the ranch."

Kade held up his hand before his mother could even let the offer flow from her lips. "Thanks, Ma, but no thanks. Dad has just about retired, and it's time you do the same. You two should buy that camper and travel, the way you always said you would."

"He can hire a nanny," Kaeden offered.

"Oh God, and wind up on the six o'clock news, with all the weirdos in the world today?" Lisha retorted.

"Yes, make me have to catch a case, Kade," Kaitlyn added.

"I'm not saying go find any jackrabbit on the street," Kaeden countered. "There are many reputable agencies that thoroughly screen their employees."

"Oh, like the Catholic Church?" Kaitlyn flung back.

Kade released a heavy breath as nearly his entire family began a full-blown debate on the pros and cons of hiring a nanny. He loved his family. He cherished them, but . . . they could be overwhelming at times.

He slid his hands into the pockets of his Dickies and shook his head a bit as he looked heavenward and licked his lips.

"I have just the solution for you, brother-in-law," said Bianca.

Kade lowered his eyes and then looked into Bianca's smiling face. "Give it to me, sister-in-law."

"Garcelle," she said simply, with a subtle lift of her rounded shoulders.

"Garcelle?" asked Kade.

"Garcelle," she said again, with finality.

Kade squinted his eyes as he thought of Garcelle.

Having worked the last year couple of years as Kahron and Bianca's part-time cook and housekeeper, Garcelle Santos had already proven herself to be trustworthy and loyal. She was the daughter of Kahron's foreman—someone else who had proven to be a valuable asset to his brother's business. And although Kade had treated the woman with suspicion and some disdain during their first meeting, he had come to see just how very wrong he was.

Kadina already loved Garcelle. Everyone did. She was more of a family friend than an employee. She was perfect for Kadina.

Kade nodded. "Garcelle," he stated, with equal finality.

"Good," Bianca agreed, with a wink, before turning and walking back to the rest of the family.

Garcelle. Yes, she is just what I need, thought Kade.

The seemingly innocent thought startled him. He shook his head as if to clear it. *I mean she's just what Kadina needs,* he corrected himself before stepping forward to rejoin his family.

2

Today was the very first day Garcelle wasn't worried about any of her usual daily grind: a full load of nursing classes, the part-time job as Kade and Bianca's housekeeper and cook, and her involuntary job as the housekeeper and cook for her brood of male family members.

Spring session was officially over, and with it, her first year at the University of South Carolina's Salkahatchie campus in Walterboro. She was studying to be a licensed practical nurse and had every intention of going back eventually to become a registered nurse. At twenty-six, she was starting to focus on a life with a career and not just a job. She was determined to put behind her her days of working at fast-food restaurants and gas stations. As much as she loved working for Kahron and Bianca, she knew, without a doubt, it wasn't what she would be doing for the rest of her life.

Without any summer classes, she was going to enjoy not having to worry about tests, books, or anything else college related. Instead, she wanted to find another part-time job so that she could save money for the fall session of school. Garcelle was on a one-woman mission to graduate without owing one red cent in school loans.

But the job search could—and would—wait one day.

Garcelle took one last leisurely stretch in the middle of her full-sized bed before she flung back the covers. Her bedroom was alive with her fiery spirit. Every bit of the room was in shades of vibrant red, which gave just the jolt of energy she needed to start her day. As much as she had decorated her small bedroom with care, Garcelle couldn't wait until she was in her own apartment. Right now all her money went for school, and she just couldn't afford rent, electricity, and a phone bill. She didn't even have a cell phone.

The three-bedroom, short, double-wide mobile home was not large enough for her large family, which consisted of her father; her two uncles; her younger brother, Paco; and herself. They were already using the den as a spare bedroom. If her older sister, Marisol, hadn't married and moved to Texas with her husband, the house would really be cramped.

"Soon," she promised herself, knowing the move would be just as good for the rest of her family as it would be for her. As soon as she graduated, she was striking out alone.

She rolled out of bed with more energy than she actually felt. As she pulled her hair up into a loose topknot, she left her bedroom and made her way to the bathroom for a quick brush of her teeth and wash of her face. Her stomach rumbled at the thought of the stewed chicken and *mangu* she'd made yesterday. The mashed plantain dish was a staple in her native Dominican Republic. It was as ordinary to Dominicans as mashed potatoes were to Americans.

Dressed in the men's boxers she had worn to bed and a worn and torn wifebeater T-shirt, Garcelle released a stream of fiery expletives as she walked down the short hall to the living room. "Pigs," she exclaimed, doing a full spin in the center of the small room. Dirty dishes were on the coffee table. Dirty socks, with the bottoms almost as black as the soles of shoes, had been flung about like confetti. The television blared a rerun of one of those racy *telenovelas* on the Spanish network. The place looked like one big mess, and unfortunately, her name was written all over cleaning it up.

All thoughts of lounging over breakfast and catching up on TiVoed episodes of *Ugly Betty* and *Grey's Anatomy* were put aside . . . for now. She opened the front door but left the glass screen door closed as a South Carolina summer wind blew in against her thighs.

She used the remote to turn the television channel to music videos, and then she snatched up each piece of discarded dirty clothing and slammed it into the laundry basket she now held against her hip. "Everything I Can't Have" by Robin Thicke began to play, and Garcelle easily slipped into subtle dance movements as she moved about the living room. Her anger began to fade, and the infectious music, with its Latin beat, made her drop the basket to the floor and shake the topknot from her hair as she began to salsa, with a wicked smile on her full lips.

"Whoo," she screamed, flinging her head back as sweat dripped down the valley between her small breasts. She worked her hips and then kicked her leg high like she had an audience. Garcelle loved to dance, and dancing always made her feel . . . *muy caliente.*

It was hard to deny that dancing was so much like making love. Sweaty bodies. Pounding hearts. Gyrating hips. Plus, she had those strong and thick thighs, which seemed to massage her intimate lips as she did the traditional Latin dances she favored. Once, when she was at Kahron and Bianca's wedding reception, lost in the groove and sipping on margaritas, she almost danced herself to a climax. *Although* that night she didn't know if it was just the dance or the sexy, silver-haired man who watched her as she danced for him. She felt her cheeks warm at the memory.

Since months had passed since her last relationship, and there was nothing in her immediate future to sate any forbidden desires, she twirled her hips one last time. *Give it up. Turn it loose, chica* she told herself.

Garcelle pulled her hair back into a topknot and pulled the clinging T-shirt from her pert breasts and suddenly hard nipples. She grabbed the basket of clothes to toss into the wash and then retraced her steps to gather up the dishes and load them in the dishwasher.

Thankfully, the kitchen was in much better shape, since everyone loved to eat in front of the TV. In no time at all, she'd straightened it up, then grabbed a can of apple juice from the fridge.

The laughter of playing children drifted in through the open kitchen window. She squinted her eyes against the sun as she watched them over the rim of the can. They were enjoying a game of kickball in the large field in the center of the trailer park. Usually at this time of the day, the trailer park was quiet. Then again, the kids were usually in school.

"Life was so simple then," she whispered into her can, thinking of her own childhood back in Santo Domingo.

Back then the divide between the rich and the poor had not been so noticeable, but with every year she grew, things became clearer. She began to understand the lack of opportunities her parents spoke of. She began to desire the same things they wanted. Although she would miss the Caribbean, in her eyes, America became the prize.

Her family had moved to America seven short years ago. It was the typical search for the American dream of getting a big slice of the pie. Of course, the reality was far less grandiose than their dreams of big houses and even bigger salaries, but her parents had made a good life for themselves in South Carolina. Her father's experience working on farms back in Santo Domingo had helped land him the job on Kahron's ranch. Soon her parents saved up some money and bought the mobile home— the first piece of property they'd ever owned. Her mother bore the son Garcelle's father had always wanted . . . especially after two daughters. Life was good for them.

Her mother's death just two years later had seemed a mockery. Paco had only been a year old. Marisol had already met and married her husband, Juan, and was living in Texas. Garcelle had just graduated high school. Her father had just landed the job as Kahron's foreman.

Garcelle looked over her shoulder at the large portrait of her mother on the wall, over the small, round dining table. She felt comforted by her smiling face.

Many people had balked when her father moved the portrait into the kitchen, but Garcelle understood that for Maria Santos, the kitchen had been the heart of the home. It was the perfect spot for her to continue watching over her family.

"I miss you, Mother," she said softly in Spanish. "We all miss you."

Deliberately brushing away the sadness, Garcelle tilted her head back as she swallowed down the last of the juice. She tossed the can into the trash as she left the kitchen and made her way back to her bedroom.

Garcelle was at the small convenience store down the road from the trailer park, searching for canned pinto beans, when she felt that she was being stared at. She glanced to the right and then directed her gaze downward. One pair of huge brown eyes looked up at her from the mocha cherub face of a six- or seven-year-old.

The little girl tugged at her heart. "*Hola, ángel,*" said Garcelle.

"Are you Beyoncé?" the little one asked.

Garcelle tossed her head back a bit and laughed. "No, I'm not Beyoncé," she told her, with her heavy Spanish accent.

"You look like her," the little girl answered simply.

"Really? I think I look more like Shakira, *ángel,*" she said softly.

The little girl's face scrunched up in obvious confusion. "Who?" she asked, tilting her head to the side as she bit her bottom lip.

"She's a singer from Colombia," Garcelle told her as she slid her hands into the tight back pockets of her jeans.

"Ooh," she said as if enlightened. "My cousin Cootie lives in Columbia."

It was Garcelle's turn to scrunch up her face.

"Kimani? Where are you?" a woman called out from the front of the small store.

"That's my mother. Bye, Beyoncé look-alike," the little girl called over her shoulder before skipping away.

"*Adiós.*" Garcelle just shook her head as she renewed her search for the pinto beans.

"That man is too damn fine."

"Yes, girl. Lord, why you make him so fine?"

"Girl, he makes the poom-poom go whoomp-whoomp."

Garcelle's thick eyebrows arched a bit as she heard two women in the next aisle laugh like they were watching a comedienne do stand-up. Their voices sounded familiar. Holtsville was a small town, and she didn't doubt that she knew them.

"And he all up in that big ole house, just begging a sistah to come take care of him."

"Well, you gone have to beat this sistah to the punch, 'cause I got the lips and the hips to get the job done."

Garcelle had to admit that they had her interest piqued. She was sure they sounded like Rita and Pita Kooley—a set of loud and rambunctious twins, who lived in the trailer next door to her family's. Between the two of them, they had six children piled into a three-bedroom single-wide.

"I've had my eye on that man since we were in high school."

"Hell, me, too. Matter of fact, I'll take any one of them brothers."

"You got that right."

Garcelle moved down the aisle to get into the short line for the cashier. When she heard the voices come up behind her, she gave in to temptation and glanced back. Pita and Rita, just like she'd thought.

Both were dressed in skintight leggings and tank tops that revealed their curvy frames. It was quite obvious they knew their assets and weren't afraid to show them.

"You know we ain't the only ones with our eyes on him," Pita said.

"Him moving back to his house is a sign and a half that he's ready to stop mourning and ready to start living, baby," Rita added.

Garcelle sat the can on the chipped and scratched wooden counter as she dug in her back pocket for her money.

"Are y'all talkin' 'bout Kade Strong?" Keisha, the cashier, asked. Her shoulder-length hair was dyed the shocking shade of royal blue.

Garcelle's heart slammed against her chest like a head-on collision. Kade. Visions of her crimson dress swirling around her like a parasol flashed before her, followed by an image of Kade moving closer to the dance floor to watch her, with the most intense eyes.

"Sure are," Pita said in a drawn-out voice.

Keisha paused for a second, with a faraway look in her eyes. "I heard he's moving back into his house."

"Sure is," Rita assured her. "But all these heifers thinking 'bout plit-plotting might as well fall back, 'cause I got some tricks up my sleeve for that brotha."

Pita sucked air between her teeth. "Well, chick, you ain't the only one with some tricks . . . or treats."

The ladies all laughed together as Garcelle accepted her change and the brown paper bag holding her can of beans. She left them gossiping animatedly as she stepped out of the store.

Kade moved back in his house, she thought as she dropped the bag into the basket attached to her ten-speed bike. *Good for him.*

Anyone who wasn't *muy loco* could see that Kade was an attractive man. During their first meeting that day at Kahron's house, Garcelle had found her pulse racing—even as she put him in his place about insinuating that she was a lowly thief. Never had she wanted to slap a man and kiss him all at once.

While working for Kahron and spending time around the family, she'd learned Kade's story, and her heart ached for the man, who seemed lost and withdrawn without his wife. The only time he seemed to open up was around his family . . . especially Kadina. He was one man who loved and adored his daughter. That was one thing that had softened her heart toward the man, who could seem very cold and distant.

One thing the crazy women had said was true: his decision to move back into his beautiful home was a sign that he was prepared to move on . . . the best thing that he could do under the circumstances.

Garcelle rode the bike down the long and bumpy dirt road leading to the trailer park. She enjoyed riding her bike as long as her destination wasn't too far. Otherwise, she flew around town in her old Volkswagen Cabriolet.

She was just turning into their front yard when a black Chevy Caprice slowed to a halt beside her.

The darkly tinted driver's side window went down, but Garcelle didn't need to see the driver to know it was her ex, Joaquin Consuelo.

Garcelle gave him an eye roll and continued riding on.

His car continued to roll slowly beside her.

She slammed on the brakes. "What do you want, Joaquin?" she snapped as she put her feet on the ground and balanced the bike between her legs.

"You," he answered simply.

Garcelle arched her eyebrows, with plenty of attitude, as she felt her anger rise. "When you had me, you wanted other women, remember?" she asked, her accent thickening with her irritation.

"Garcelle, I never cheated on you," he said, placing the car in park.

A year into their relationship, Joaquin, through hard work, had saved up enough money to start his own landscaping business. And it flourished quickly. More money than he was used to started to roll in, and things between Garcelle and him started to change.

"No, you just broke up with me because you didn't want to be tied down," she snapped. "The *dinero* and your business went to your head. The women were crawling all over you, and you wanted anything in a skirt. What? The grass—or should I say ass—wasn't better, like you thought?"

"I just wanted to check on you and see how you're doing."

"I'm doing fine," she told him, climbing back onto her bike.

"You looking fine as hell, too," he said, his eyes taking in her long, shapely legs and round buttocks in the cutoff jean shorts she wore. "Damn fine, *bonita*."

Garcelle hated that her pulse raced. She absolutely hated it.

Joaquin was gorgeous. He had angular features, a tall frame, and those dark and swarthy Marc Anthony type of gorgeous looks. Garcelle had fallen for him hard the first time he asked for her number. They had been inseparable during the last year of the relationship, and his sudden declaration two months ago that he wanted his freedom had rocked Garcelle's world. She was just starting to feel fully recovered. She was just starting to feel like the old Garcelle.

No matter how fine he was. No matter how good she *knew* the loving was. No matter how much she used to miss him and crave him like a drug. There was no more Joaquin and Garcelle. They were *finito*.

Garcelle pushed off on her bike. "*Adiós*, Joaquin," she called over her shoulder.

"Garcelle—"

"*A-di-ós!*"

Garcelle cruised into the front yard, jumped off her bike, and parked it next to her car, which was in dire need of a paint job and some other repairs. It was over twenty years old, but she loved it because she'd bought it with her own hard-earned money.

She barely took a second to grab her bag from the basket before she dashed into the house. She didn't even waste her time to see if Joaquin had left her alone as she'd ordered. She had a dinner of chili con carne to finish before her *familia* got home for the evening. Although she said she was tired of taking care of them, Garcelle knew they deserved a home-cooked meal after a hard day of work at the Circle S Ranch. Even little Paco would spend his summer days helping out.

Garcelle added the beans to the chili and stirred it slowly before she tasted the broth. She added a little more crushed red pepper and salt before she replaced the lid and turned the electric burner on low. She was just gathering the ingredients for a quick corn bread when there was a knock at the front door.

Thinking it was a persistent Joaquin, Garcelle slammed the spoon on the counter, sending bits of the cornmeal batter flying. She turned and stormed out of the kitchen on her long, shapely legs and snatched the front door open. "Are you stupid or just crazy . . . ?"

The rest of her tirade trailed off into nothing as she looked up into the surprised face of Kade Strong.

Garcelle rose up on her toes to look over his shoulder. There was no sign of Joaquin or his car. Dropping back down on her feet, she gave him a weak smile. "Sorry. I thought you were someone else," she explained, with a faint smile, as she leaned against the open door.

"I can come back," he offered, sliding his large and strong hands into the pockets of his tan Dickies pants.

Garcelle reached out to lightly touch his arm. Her eyes didn't miss the way he flinched slightly from her touch. She instantly withdrew her hand. "How can I help you?" she asked coolly even as she noticed the descending sun illuminating off the big silver curls in his hair.

"You could pretend my being here doesn't annoy you," he said in a dry tone.

Garcelle bit back the smile that threatened to spread across her face. "Well, hello, Kade Strong. It is so splendiferous to see you on this glorious day. I was just saying how wonderful it would be to see Kade Strong, and here you are. I'm so lucky," she said in a loud, exaggerated voice, her tongue rolling over his last name.

He smiled. It was slow and even kind of hesitant, but it was a smile, nonetheless. "That's some big-time overkill, but I'll take it over the sour attitude you give me most times."

"Being called a thief makes you, how do you say . . . *sour*," she told him as she crossed her arms over her chest.

"Damn, you sure can hold a grudge," he balked, with an incredulous expression, as he looked down at her.

Garcelle looked up at him, with a soft smile, which she didn't bother to hide. "No, I just like to give you a hard time, Kade Strong," she admitted.

He pulled his hand from his pocket and extended it to her. "Truce?" he asked.

He really is a beautiful man, she thought as she slid her hand into his. "Truce," she agreed just as warm shots of electricity radiated across her hand and up her arm to harden her nipples into tight buds. Garcelle looked down at his bronzed skin against the soft caramel of her own. The warmth continued to spread across her body with ease.

She snatched her hand away.

"Something wrong?" he asked.

"Uh, no. Uh-uh. Everything's good," she said, looking up at him as she wiped a sudden flood of sweat from her forehead. "How can I help you, Kade?"

"I'm moving back into my house this week—"

Garcelle snorted. "So I heard," she said dryly.

"Excuse me?" he asked.

Garcelle forced a smile. "Nothing."

Kade shifted his weight on the porch and cleared his throat. "Anyway, I need help with Kadina this summer, and Bianca said you might be interested, since you only work for them like once a week for half a day."

"Like a *niñera*?" she asked.

"A what?" Kade asked.

Garcelle laughed. "You call it a . . . a nanny. Sometimes it's easier for me to say certain things in Spanish."

"It's funny that you look black, but you're Mexican."

Garcelle rolled her eyes. "I'm Dominican. Latinos come from more places than just Mexico or Puerto Rico. Okay?"

Kade licked his lips and looked apologetic. "I didn't mean any disrespect."

Garcelle laughed softly as she reached up to lightly pat his cheek like he was a child . . . a big, six-foot five-inch, muscular, good-looking child. "Don't worry. We'll have all summer, while I'm watching Kadina, to teach you more about Latinos, Kade Strong."

"So you'll take the job?" he asked as his eyes locked with hers.

"*Sí*," she answered, with a nod.

"Good," he said, with a nod of his own. "Can you start Monday?"

"*Sí*."

"Great. Bye then, Garcelle." Kade turned to leave.

"*Adiós*, Kade Strong." Her eyes drifted down his strong back to his tight buttocks in the uniform pants he wore. *Not bad. Not bad at all.*

Kade turned suddenly.

Garcelle jerked her eyes up to his face as a warm blush flooded her cheeks.

"One more thing, Garcelle," he said, his eyes sparkling with humor. "Are you always going to call me by my full name?"

Garcelle stepped back and began to close the front door. "*Sí,*" she said playfully before closing the door.

She leaned back against the closed door and breathed out through pursed lips as she waited for her heartbeat to slow down.

3

One Week Later

"¡Uno . . . dos . . . tres . . . cuatro . . . cinco . . . seis . . . siete . . . ocho . . . nueve . . . diez!"

Garcelle smiled with pleasure in the rearview mirror as she looked at Kadina, who sat buckled in the backseat of her car. "Very good. You learn so very quickly. Your father will be proud when you recite the numbers for him when he gets home tonight."

Kadina nodded as she sipped from the bottle of fruit punch she held. "He already says I'm starting to talk like you. I'm picking up your ashent," she said, with pride.

Garcelle laughed. "That's ac-cent," she stressed.

Kadina laughed as well. "Yup, *that's* what he said."

Garcelle steered her Cabrio carefully as she drove them to Kahron and Bianca's to deliver the meals she'd cooked for them at Kade's. She would clean the house and warm up one of the dishes for their dinner.

"I like going to Uncle Kahron and Auntie Bianca's," Kadina said.

Garcelle's eyes shifted momentarily up to the rearview mirror. "Hershey, right?"

Kadina nodded. "I love that lazy dog. She always lays her head on my lap and then falls asleep. I don't mind that, until she farts in her sleep. Whoo. Talk about rotten eggs and stinky feet."

Garcelle laughed. "That bad, huh?"

"Worst."

In just one short week, Gacelle had fallen even harder for the little girl with long ponytails and a toothy smile. "Remind me to stay upwind of Hershey," she quipped as she parked her Cabrio in front of the house.

"I will," Kadina promised, with a giggle.

Garcelle lifted the box holding the containers of food from the cracked backseat. "Do you want to go horseback riding now while I work?" she asked as they climbed the stairs together.

Kadina held up her latest Cheetah Girls book. "I'll just read and wait for you to get done. That cool?"

"That's cool with me."

They walked into the house, and the coolness of the central air felt good after the sweltering Carolina summer heat. "I wonder if Uncle Kahron likes all the changes Auntie Bianca made around here?" Kadina asked.

Garcelle hoisted the box higher as they moved into the kitchen. "It looks much better, so he should love it," she said as she began to place the containers in the fridge.

The masculine décor of dark tones, large leather furnishings, and even larger electronics had been replaced with a more contemporary and comfortable style. It was a good mix of colors and textures so that a woman, man, or family could be comfortable in their surroundings.

Kadina settled onto the new window seat at the rear of the kitchen, but she never opened the book she held in her hand. Instead, her eyes were focused out the window. "Aunt Bianca is good for Uncle Kahron," she said suddenly.

"Seems that way," Garcelle told her as she emptied the container of beef stew into a large pot on the stove.

"She makes him happy."

Garcelle stirred the stew as she looked over her shoulder at Kadina. "Yes. Being in love can make someone very, very happy."

"So if my dad fell in love, would that make him happy again?" Kadina asked, her voice barely above a whisper.

Garcelle bit her bottom lip as she turned the burner on low and placed the lid on the pot. She went to sit beside Kadina on the window seat. "I don't think that your dad is unhappy. He's just grieving. And that takes time, you know? You can tell that he loved your mother very much."

"Would it be wrong for him to love someone else?"

"Well, I think this is something you should talk about with your dad, sweetheart." Garcelle reached over to pat her hand comfortingly before she rose and walked back over to the sink to wash out the now-empty container.

"Garcelle?"

Garcelle turned the water off in the sink and turned to face Kadina.

Kadina shifted her gaze from the window to Garcelle. "Is it wrong for me to want him to love someone else?"

"No, no, baby, it's not wrong at all," Garcelle told her. "When my mother died, I was much older than you, but as much I missed her and as much as I knew my father missed her, too, I knew she wouldn't want him to spend the rest of his life alone. I bet your mother feels the same way. In fact, I believe she has the power from heaven to send just the right woman to him."

"Really?" Kadina asked in obvious doubt.

"Oh yes, honey. So, no dipping your little nose all up in your daddy's love life." Garcelle winked at her playfully to lighten the mood.

"You sure? 'Cause I think you might be just what my daddy needs," Kadina told her, with confidence, as she rose and crossed her slender arms over her chest.

Garcelle tossed her head and laughed until tears formed in her almond-shaped eyes. "Me?" she balked. "Oh no, baby. Nothing doing. Trust me. Your daddy and me? You are hilarious."

Kadina strolled across the kitchen. "Don't you think he's cute? *I* think he's cute."

Garcelle tossed her hair over her shoulder as she leaned her ample bottom against the counter's edge. "You know what? I will admit your papi is beyond cute."

Kadina's grin widened.

"*But*," said Garcelle.

Kadina's grin dropped quicker than a bag of weights.

Garcelle stroked her cheek. "Love you lots, Kadina, but your daddy and me? No way. No how."

Kade rode his white Appalachian horse, Star, along the outer perimeter of the herd. He used the horse and his own skill to help guide the herd to the northern area of Strong Ranch.

His muscles ached from the exertion, the sun beat down on his back and shoulders, and sweat made his clothes bond to his frame, but he loved it. He was focused on working in conjunction with his ranch hands and his brother to get the herd moved before nightfall.

He wanted to get home early tonight and actually spend some time with Kadina. He also had some more unpacking to do. Walking around a house where most of the furniture was still covered with sheets and the rooms were filled with boxes didn't give one the feeling of home, which he wanted to provide for his daughter. Plus, Garcelle had been a good sport to work later than he'd first asked so that he could get the herd shifted.

Garcelle.

Kadina filled his nights with her daily adventures with Garcelle. He smiled and shook his head at the thought of Kadina talking with Garcelle's Spanish accent. It tickled him when she called him Papi instead of Daddy. And he came home one night to find her listening to merengue music in her room.

All of that he didn't mind, but he had to draw the line at letting her loosen her ponytail to wear her hair like Garcelle or letting her learn how to belly dance like Shakira. A dance that Garcelle had demonstrated very well at Kahron and Bianca's wedding reception a couple of months ago. Very, very well.

Her hips had almost hypnotized him that night. Left, then right, and then left again. Round and around. Clockwise and then counterclockwise until he didn't even remember his steps carrying him closer to the dance floor. Closer to her.

Shaking his head for clarity, Kade motioned for one of the hands to move up and take his spot before he steered his horse over to Kahron, who was riding his own horse, Midnight. "Thanks again for helping out," Kade said as he made his horse match the trot of his brother's.

Kahron had an odd expression as he placed his signature aviator shades atop his head. "Yeah, you thanked me already. It's no problem."

"Oh yeah, that's right," Kade said, shifting his weight on the custom-made saddle.

They rode and worked the herd in silence.

Kahron dropped his shades back down over his eyes as he cleared his throat. "Something on your mind?"

Kade frowned as he brought his horse to a stop outside the fence and watched the hands steer the cattle through the open gate. "Nah," he protested.

"How's Kadina adjusting to the new house?" Kahron asked.

"Pretty good, actually." Kade shielded the setting sun from his eyes with his hand. "Having Garcelle around is making the transition smoother."

Kahron nudged Midnight around. "Yeah, Garcelle is great."

Kade swallowed a lump in his throat as he steered his horse back in the direction from which they'd traveled. "Yeah . . . great."

He didn't miss the sidelong glance his brother cast him. "I'm not about to lose another housekeeper, am I?" Kahron asked, referring to his startling record of hiring—and firing—fifteen housekeepers in a very short span of time. Garcelle was number sixteen.

Kade shaped his handsome, square face into a frown. "What do you mean?"

"Not trying to steal her away for good, are you?"

Kahron squinted his eyes as he looked up at the fading sun. They took the lead, guiding the rest of the group across the grassy land.

"Man, please. We just started having civil conversations," said Kade.

"Good. Because I don't think I can take another housekeeper hunt." Kahron steered his horse to the front as they neared a narrow trail. "With Bianca working so many hours at her practice and doing her share at her father's horse ranch, we need the help."

"Everything okay with the newlyweds?" Kade asked as the trail widened, and he steered Star beside his brother.

"Just not feeling so much like typical newlyweds since we got back from our honeymoon."

Kade nodded in understanding at the long look his brother gave him. "Oh."

Kahron reined in his horse. Kade rode ahead a bit before he, too, stopped and looked over his shoulder at his brother. "What's the holdup?"

The dozen or so hands came to a stop as well. Kade frowned as Kahron waved them on. "What the hell?" Kade muttered as his brother rode back toward him.

"How in the hell do you do it?" Kahron asked before Kade could even open his mouth to question him.

"Do what?"

"Man, Bianca and I hit a dry spell for a couple of weeks, and I'm frustrated as hell. You haven't seen, smelled, touched, tasted, or been near a woman for years, and you're cool as can be!"

Kade laughed a little to shake off the slight embarrassment he felt.

"I'm not judging you or saying you need to find something to screw," said Kahron. "I'm just asking what techniques you use to get it off your mind. Help a brother out."

Kade shrugged. "Rolling over to the other side of the bed when it is cold has a way of *softening* things."

Kahron released a heavy breath. "I guess I just need to adjust to married life. Going from twice a day to once a week is a helluva switch, you know."

Kade laughed and slapped his brother on the shoulder. "I got two words for you, little brother. Cold . . . shower."

"A cold shower?" Kahron balked. "Hell, I can think of another way to get wet that don't have jack to do with a cold shower."

Kade cleared his throat playfully. "Speaking of jack—"

"I asked you to teach me something I *don't* know." Kahron flung his head back and laughed so loud that it bounced across the woods.

Garcelle and Kadina were in the den, laughing over rerun episodes of *In Living Color*, when Garcelle saw something appear at the window and then disappear. Garcelle rose from the sofa and made her way over to the window. She looked out into the ebony darkness of night. Her mouth twisted into a frown at the sight of a package, which was illuminated by the porch light.

"Is that my daddy?" Kadina asked from behind her.

"No, not yet," Garcelle called over her shoulder as she made her way to the front door to open it.

"Now what's this all about?" she asked aloud at the sight of the package and a balloon sitting there.

She bent down a bit to open the card attached to one of the curly ribbons at the base of the balloon.

Kade—
>   *Just a hint of things that will*
>   *go down between us . . . in due time.*
>   *Call me at 555-0000.*
>   *XOXOXO♥*

Garcelle slapped the small card closed, with an eye roll. She straightened back up to her full height and eyed the pink and white box as she crossed her arms over her chest. *I wonder what is in that box.*

She was just reminding herself that it wasn't her box to open when Kade's SUV pulled in front of the house. Her eyes shifted from the box, and she watched him climb the stairs to the porch.

Nearly every inch of his uniform and his Timberland boots were dusty. Sweat had thinned the fullness from his curls—curls that were now plastered against his head. There was a streak of something dark and caked across his nose.

Despite all of that, the man's good looks could not be denied. Like it or not, her pulse raced, and she felt something electric touch every part of her body.

"Is that for you?" he asked as he reached the top step.

Garcelle shook her head. "It's for you," she told him softly as she lifted her hands and twisted her hair up into a knot.

"Me?" he said in obvious surprise. He squatted down and took the lid off the box.

Garcelle leaned forward to peer into the box as well. She made a face of disgust.

"Damn," Kade said in a drawn-out fashion as he lifted a mini-whip and massage oil out of the box of tricks.

"Tricks from a trick," Garcelle muttered under her breath. She was glad Kadina hadn't come out and found the box first. How would she explain the gargantuan chocolate dildo nested in the bottom of the box?

"Huh?" Kade asked, looking up at her as he dropped the items he held back into the box.

Garcelle shook her head and feigned confusion. "Nothing."

"Is this from you?" he asked as he rose to his full height.

Garcelle cocked a brow. "No disrespect intended, Kade Strong, but you must be out your—"

Kade held up his hands. "Why don't I just read the card before you flip?"

"Yes. Do that," she told him, with attitude.

Kade actually chuckled before he read the card and then tore it in half. He scooped up the box. "You want any of this before I toss it?" he asked.

Garcelle held up a hand.

"It's all new," he joked, with a twinkle in his warm brown eyes, which lit up his face.

Garcelle almost dropped four of her fingers.

Kade laughed as he made his way down the stairs, with the balloon floating in the air behind him. Without hesitation or a pause in his movements, he dumped all of it into the large garbage container sitting in the front of the house.

Garcelle was surprised by the move. She bit her bottom lip as she watched him make his way back up the steps and onto the porch. "Didn't you want your . . . gifts?" she asked him, her accent heavy.

Kade shook his head as he came to a stop in front of her. "If I was looking to get involved with a woman—which I'm not—it wouldn't be one who sends a man sex toys."

Garcelle nodded in understanding.

Kade moved past her to walk into the house. He paused in the doorway, and Garcelle looked up at him. There were just inches between them. Inches that were infinitely filled with power.

"Thanks so much for helping out with Kadina," he told her in that masculine voice that was everything good: a hot toddy during a bad cold, great sex, sweet and hot double chocolate, a foot massage after a hard day of work, winning the lottery. . . .

Garcelle swallowed a lump in her throat. "You're welcome," she said as she fought off her awareness of him.

"Do you want me to follow you home?" he asked, as he'd done every evening since she'd taken the job.

"No, I'll be fine. I'll call, like always, to let you know I got home okay."

"Good."

"I better be going," she said, turning to walk into the house.

"Garcelle."

She turned at the sound of him saying her name. Her eyes locked with his. "¿Sí?"

"I was only joking earlier," he said, with a smile. "I didn't ever think you sent that box to me. Trust me."

Garcelle nodded and smiled playfully. "I didn't think you were crazy."

Kade flung his head back and laughed, and the

light from the porch bounced off of his silver curls. "You don't bite your tongue, do you?"

She shook her head. "Never."

They fell into a comfortable silence.

"Listen, I better warn you," she said suddenly. "The ladies feel like you're open for business since you moved back in your house. Your little gift tonight is just the start of it. You are the talk of Holtsville."

Kade looked disbelieving. "Me?" he asked, pointing to himself.

Garcelle shook her head. "Don't pretend like you don't know you're cute, Kade Strong."

His eyes locked on her, and she saw them fill with hesitation.

"I'm not feeling you like that," she balked, reaching up to pinch his arm. She tried not to notice the steel beneath her fingertips. "In fact, I'm probably one of the few single women in Holtsville who *ain't* on the prowl."

Kade sat down on the top step of the porch. In the quiet, the sounds of night creatures echoed loudly. He dropped his face into his hands before he wiped his eyes and then dragged his long fingers through his soft hair. His eyes were troubled as he looked up at the full moon, which seemed three times its normal size.

Garcelle moved from the doorway to sit on the top step, beside him. She licked her lips as she knocked her leg against his. "There's nothing wrong with not wanting to get over your wife. I think it's beautiful how much you loved—"

"Love," he stressed.

"Right." Garcelle touched his arm lightly. "My father hasn't remarried since my mother passed away, and it's been close to five years," she told him. "Now,

I won't say that I don't want him to find love again, but it has to be in his own time . . . just like you."

Kade shrugged. "I'm just sick of people making me feel like I'm crazy out my ass because I'm not out sexing women and acting a fool. Damn, can't a brotha just chill?"

Garcelle nodded, but her mind was momentarily stuck on something else. *Did he admit he hasn't had sex since his wife died?* Garcelle pursed her lips. *I feel for the woman he drops all that pressure on.*

"Most men would probably head trip off the females chasing them, but it's not what I need right now, for sure," said Kade.

Garcelle bumped her shoulder against his. "Don't worry. I got your back, and those hoochies and hags are gonna have to get through me," she said, pointing to her chest, as Kade dropped his head and laughed.

"You don't look like much of a bodyguard . . . for me, anyway," he said as he turned his face to look at her.

Garcelle felt breathless. Kade really was a good-looking man, with his square, angular features and caramel complexion, which the sun had deepened to a bronze. His eyes were deep set, and so very intense, above sharp and high cheekbones. His features were hard and handsome, in perfect contrast to his soft and curly hair.

"Garcelle?"

"Huh?" she asked, her eyes focusing in on his.

"Thanks for the talk," he said. "I never had a female friend—besides Reema."

She forced a smile. "That's me. Your buddy," she joked, even as the disappointment she felt surprised her.

4

Two Weeks Later

"See, Daddy, we're late for church," Kadina scolded him as she double-checked her ponytail in the passenger-side window.

"God will understand," Kade told her as he turned his Expedition onto the unpaved driveway of the Holtsville Baptist Church. Cars filled the yard, and Kade had to park near the ditch running along the side of the road.

They made their way inside, and Kade saw that his usual seats in the row with his family were taken.

"Psst . . . psst."

Kade turned his head to find Portia Klinton, an old classmate and the ex-wife of one of the men from his hunting club, patting the empty seat next to her in the pew. She had "gotten saved" a few weeks ago, and everyone mockingly called her Sister Portia because she seemed to be saved only on Sundays. Every other day of the week, she did plenty to repent for.

Kade waved and kept on moving.

He saw his brother Kaeden trying to discreetly get his attention near the front. Kade gripped Kadina's hand tighter and headed that way. Feeling like all eyes were resting on him, Kade was glad when they finally were in their seats.

As the church service continued on, Kade became more and more confused. Wherever he happened to rest his eyes, a woman smiled, winked, waved, or even blew kisses to him! Just when he thought he had to have imagined it, another woman would make her presence known to him. After Hazel Rogers, a divorcée with six kids—all under the age of seven—gave him a more than friendly smile, Kade focused his eyes and his full attention on the minister.

The weirdness continued after church. He could have sworn he saw the twins, Pita and Rita, shoving people out of the way to head in his direction. Kade rushed Kadina out of the church, behind Kaeden.

Everyone mingled outside, on the church grounds, and Kadina went running over to Kade's parents as soon as she spotted them. Kade and Kaeden followed at a slower space.

"Everything going good at the house?" Kaeden asked as he removed his rimless spectacles to clean them.

Kade towered over his brother by nearly four inches and had to look down at him as he answered. "Still have some unpacking to do, but I'm glad to be home."

"Kadina like it?"

"She says she does, and she talks about her mother more . . . asking lots of questions and remembering things about Reema," Kade told him, with a smile.

"She was a special woman."

Kade paused in his steps. "Yes, she was."

Kaeden nodded. "There wasn't a better whist player around—"

"Uh, excuse me, gentlemen."

Kade and Kaeden turned to find Ollie Freehold standing behind them, with a big smile. "How you doing, Ms. Ollie?" Kade asked the sixty-something church secretary.

"Blessed all day, every day. Amen," she replied.

"Yes, ma'am," the brothers said in unison.

"Kade, I wanted to talk to you about hosting a shooting match as a fund-raiser for the church," said Ms. Ollie.

Kaeden smacked Kade on the back. "I'll let y'all talk business then and excuse myself."

Kade glared at his brother's retreating back as he felt himself cornered by Ms. Ollie.

Kaeden chuckled as he walked across the church grounds, toward where his family stood. His stomach growled, and he couldn't wait to taste whatever his mother was serving up for Sunday dinner. Being a bachelor, Kaeden rarely got a home-cooked meal, and when he did, it was at his parents'. His high-tech kitchen still looked as spotless and new as the day he moved into his town house. Of course, to meet his Mrs. Right, he had to get more going on in his life than just his work.

Most of his time was spent with facts and figures—numerical and not feminine. Growing up, his brothers had joked he was the nerd of the family. The safe one. The cautious one. The nonphysical one. The nonfarming one. The nervous one.

It was always a joke that he was the spitting image of Kahron, but they were as different as night and day. Being allergic to everything under the sun had a way of making a small boy find things to do other than be outside. And being the only person in the family to avoid the outdoors had taught him often and early how to be comfortable being alone.

He felt the heavy pollen in the air tickle his eyes, nose, and throat. He lifted his glasses to rub his eyes and gave in to a sneeze that rose fast. He tried to fight using the inhaler in his suit pocket but eventually gave in, hurrying to put it back in his pocket as soon as he was done.

At the sound of a flirty and feminine laugh, Kaeden turned his head. His heart hammered, and he instantly felt his palms sweat. He paused, and he nervously licked his lips as his eyes locked on *her* through his spectacles.

Jade Prince.

She was surrounded by four men, who all were just as captivated by her as he was. He watched as she reached out to lightly touch the arm of one of the guys as she spoke to him. She flung her head back and laughed, exposing the smooth dark brown of her neck.

In his mind, everything about her moved in slow motion. Her bright smile. The wind blowing in the medium-length curls of her jet-black hair. The flutter of long and curly eyelashes. The way her dress clung to her curvy, full shape.

She was woman. All woman. Curvy enough to compete with a glass Coke bottle. Full enough to be held tightly by a man. Soft enough to make that lucky man sigh at the very feel of her body pressed against his.

Kaeden wished he could be that man. When it came to Jade, he felt like a character in *The Wiz*: if he only had the nerve. Chancing one last look at her,

Kaeden forced himself to keep on moving. A woman like Jade Prince would never take a second look at a guy like him. He had long since dealt with that fact.

"Well, who put the honey on your brother to draw all those bees?" his mother asked as Kaeden strolled up to his family.

Kaeden turned and looked over his shoulder. His eyes widened at the fifteen or so women circling around Kade. His brother looked like a deer caught in headlights from *both* directions.

"Whether he wants to be or not, looks like our big brother is back on the market," Kahron quipped from behind Kaeden.

"Oh, Jesus, is that Nettie Barnes gazing up in Kade's face with her fifty-year-old self?" Kael said, sounding annoyed.

"She's just hitting her prime, Pops," Bianca added.

"Well, I would want a stepmother, *not* a step-grandmother," Kadina said, with a definite frown.

The entire Strong bunch laughed.

Garcelle stroked her brother Paco's head, which rested in her lap, as they watched television. Her father was napping in the recliner across the room, and her two uncles were in the backyard, playing dominoes with a couple of their neighbors. The house was quiet, and it felt good just spending time with her little brother. Every day he was changing. She was already chasing off fast and hot little thirteen- and fourteen-year-old girls who were flirting with him because they thought he was older than he looked.

She knew that soon he would be the one doing the

chasing. She smiled at the thought of Paco with a girl-friend. It seemed like it was just yesterday that he was a chubby toddler that she loved to rock to sleep.

Paco used to love strawberry ice cream on a cone. He would lick the ice cream and then talk to it in that gibberish talk of toddlers. It was if he was in love with that cone, and he was that way each and every time he had one.

"Paco, do you remember how much you used to love ice cream cones?" she asked.

Her answer was a quiet snore that got louder as it lengthened. She kissed her two fingertips and then pressed them to his cheek. It was a special gesture that she'd done ever since he was just a baby.

She eased his head off her lap and rose to walk into the kitchen. She double-checked their lunch of roasted pork and yellow rice before she glanced out the window. Her uncles' music was blaring and mingled with their and their neighbors' raised voices as they played dominoes like their lives depended on it. They were making quite a ruckus. The trailers were not that far apart, and with the blurred line between one person's backyard and a neighbor's front yard, she was glad everyone in the trailer park got along so well.

She glanced over to the next row of trailers and saw that her friend Marta was home from her job as a housekeeper at the Holiday Inn. Garcelle reached in the back pocket of her jean gauchos. She counted out fifty dollars.

She wasn't at all surprised when the telephone rang just moments later. "What's up, Marta?"

"You know what's up. Get your wide hip ass over here."

Garcelle just laughed as she hung up the phone.

She walked out the back door, throwing a wave to her uncles and the hand to their friends, whose mouths started to drool as soon as they spotted her.

"Man, hook me up with your niece," one of them said.

"What the hell this look like? Match.com or some shit?" she heard her Uncle Anthony say. "Just play dominoes, man."

Garcelle walked up the dirt road circling the entire trailer park. She came up on the big field in the center of the park, where the kids were playing kick-ball.

"Garcelle, Paco home?" one of the kids yelled out.

"He's sleeping, but go wake him up," she yelled back.

She cut across the rear of the field and walked into Marta's yard and past her new Ford Escort. She was just opening the door to Marta's single-wide mobile home when their friend Tasha's bright pink Cadillac whipped into the yard. Garcelle waited and held the door open for her.

"Whassup, Beyoncé?" Tasha teased as she climbed the wooden steps. She was a short, full-figured girl who was not afraid in the least to wear a pair of short shorts and a tube top.

"*Hola, chicas. ¿Cómo estás?*" Garcelle joked back as they walked into Marta's house.

"Girl, I told you don't be speaking no Spanish to me," said Tasha.

Garcelle just laughed.

Marta and her sister Francesca were already sitting around the small, round table in her kitchen. Marta shuffled the deck of cards she held as she looked up at them through a plume of cigarette smoke. "Poochie's on the way," she told them.

Garcelle took her seat and slapped her fifty-dollar stake on the table. This was her one recreation. A Sunday afternoon chilling with her crazy friends, complete with some light beer, storytelling, joke cracking, and a good ole deck of fifty-two, was just what she needed.

They heard the bass of a car system beat against the walls of the trailer. "Here comes Poochie," Tasha said, after peeking out the window. "She and Tank must be back together, 'cause he just dropped her off."

Marta pulled harder on her cigarette and rolled her eyes, with a string of Spanish expletives. "I guess we gone hear 'Tank this' and 'Tank that' all damn night."

"She got her little boy with her?" Garcelle asked.

"No," said Tasha.

"Thank God, 'cause he is bad as hell," Garcelle said just before the front door opened and Poochie strolled in.

"Lookey here, Garcelle. I got some new tricks for your ass today, baby," Poochie said as she slid into a chair at the table. "You *ain't* walking out with all the money this time."

Garcelle picked up the cards and shuffled them, looking each of her friends in the eye. "The game is seven-card stud, and in case you *chicas* still haven't learned . . . *I'm* the one to beat."

"You boys sure you want to do this?" Kade asked as he easily handled the stallion that he was riding.

Kahron trotted up. He winked at his brother playfully before removing his chain with the cross medallion and slipping it into the back pocket of his slacks. "Scared you wrote a check that's going to bounce?" he asked as he dropped his shades down over his eyes.

Kade ignored him and looked over his shoulder as Kaleb slowly trotted his horse like he was in a parade. "Watch him now. He swears that slow and steady always wins the race," Kade joked as he shook his head.

After dinner they had all been sitting around their parents' den, telling stories of their childhood, when Kade recalled how his younger brothers had always tried—and failed—to beat him in horse racing. That led to Kade, Kaleb, and Kahron all removing their suit jackets and rolling up the sleeves of their shirts. They were going to race for old time's sake.

Their mother warned them against such foolishness. Their father told them he wanted each and every one of his horses returned just the way the boys found them or he would cut some tail *for old time's sake.*

Bianca thought they were being childish, placing the horses at risk for male pride. Even her threats to withhold her wifely duty didn't stop Kahron from wanting to beat his older brother.

So here they were.

"Hold on. I want in on this," Kaitlyn called out from behind them.

The three brothers turned their silver-haired heads and looked over their equally broad and square shoulders to see Kaitlyn racing toward them on an all-white stallion. Kaeden rode with her, with his spectacles in his hand.

Kaitlyn pulled the reins and stopped on a dime beside them, sending dirt and dust flying. The men all coughed and covered their faces with their arms as they waited for the soil to settle. "I wasn't old enough to get in on the fun, but I want a chance to whup all my brothers' butts . . . well, except for Kaeden. No offense, big brother."

Kaeden cleaned his specs with a handkerchief from his back pocket. "None taken," he said, with a wheeze-like cough.

"You okay?" Kade asked, with his powerful eyes on his brother.

"I'm fine," Kaeden snapped as he slipped his glasses back on.

Kahron and Kade shared a long look.

"Okay, Kaeden, you can be the judge, like always," Kaleb said as he tried to settle down the black Arabian he rode. "You stay here, and we'll all go down to that line of trees, our starting point."

Kaeden slid down from the horse. As soon as his feet hit the ground, the other Strong siblings rode their horses toward the spot Kaleb had pointed out.

Kade was the first one to reach the trees. "Just a little preview of what I'm 'bout to do to y'all."

"You haven't crossed the finish line yet, brother," Kahron told him.

"Damn right," Kaleb threw in.

Kaitlyn just held the reins tighter and positioned her slender frame on the saddle, with a determined look on her face.

In the distance, Kaeden raised one arm. "On your mark . . . get set . . . go!"

They all took off.

Kade rode his horse hard, rising up from the saddle as he let the animal take the lead. He passed the stretches of trees and grass drying from the heat of the sun. He could hear the hooves thundering against the ground as his siblings all vied to beat him. His heart thundered from the exhilaration of the race. Kaeden's silhouette increased in size as Kade neared him.

Risking a look back to check his competition, Kade glanced over his shoulder. Kaleb was on his heels. Kahron was coming up strong, with his shades making him look like a robot. Kaitlyn brought up the rear but was fighting to close the gap.

Kade faced forward, but his expression went from that of victory to confusion as his horse suddenly reared up and then stopped, causing his body to go flying over the horse's head. He landed on the ground, with a thud.

"Shit," he swore, with a grimace, as pain radiated across his body.

"Paco, come and eat," Garcelle called out to her brother as she left Marta's house. She counted her poker winnings as she walked into the house. *Two hundred and thirty dollars,* she told herself. She walked straight into her room and grabbed the empty pickle jar, where she kept her money until she went to the bank. She rammed the money atop the bills already crunched in there.

She loved playing poker. Joaquin had taught her how to play, and she had taken to it like a fish to water. She hated when the state outlawed those video poker machines, because it had been nothing for her to win five hundred dollars or better in one sitting. Most times when men heard she was a skilled poker player, they laughed and tried to play her like a joke . . . until she had their pockets empty or their backsides bare.

She wasn't addicted to gambling at all. In fact, she

only played with her friends on Sunday afternoons, and even then, once she lost her fifty-dollar table stake, she sat out or went home. Oh, she loved poker, but the game wasn't serious enough to cut into her money for school or make her borrow money to play.

Garcelle left her room. "You awake, Papi?" she asked her father.

Carlos laughed as he wiped his hand over his mouth. "Yes, and I'm starving," he answered.

"Coming right up," she told him over her softly rounded shoulder as she headed for the kitchen.

"Paco, wash your hands, and go and set the table," she heard her father tell her brother in Spanish.

They always ate their dinner together as a family. It was their way of honoring her mother, because family meals had been so important to her. Even when Garcelle worked late, watching Kadina, or her father and her uncles had an emergency at the ranch that held them up, no one would eat until everyone was home.

Paco set the table as Garcelle placed steaming platters of food in the center of the table. Her father came into the kitchen and walked to the back door. "Anthony and Raul," he called out to his two twenty-something younger brothers. They shared the same father, but had different mothers. Once he was settled in America, Carlos had sent for her uncles and got them the jobs at the Circle S Ranch.

Garcelle enjoyed the family banter as they talked freely and with ease in Spanish while she fixed the plates and handed one to each of the men. As their talk turned to the ranch, Garcelle immediately thought of Kade.

The women of Holtsville were on a full-blown campaign to see who would be the woman to snag the very eligible but very reluctant bachelor Kade Strong. In the two weeks since the package had been left on Kade's step, Garcelle had intercepted letters, cards, phone calls, and even more risqué packages from the single women of Holtsville, South Carolina. She swore, if she laid eyes on one more nudie shot, she would retch.

All of it smelled of man-hungry, desperate women. Not to say there wasn't a good woman out there for Kade, but so far these women, who were trying to lure him with sex, were hardly great candidates to be Kadina's stepmother. No, these women only wanted to lie up in Kade's bed and probably send Kadina to her room or outside to amuse herself.

She was the type of active and smart little girl who needed someone to talk to her and spend time with her. Take her to the parks and museums she loved. Take her to the bookstore to carefully select the next book she would read. Tell her about little boys when the time came. And do all the things women knew that a man didn't do, such as help her through her first menstrual cycle.

Kadina needed someone patient, loving, and fun like . . . Garcelle herself. Garcelle literally shook her head at the thought. She definitely was not throwing herself in the running to be the second Mrs. Kade Strong. In the last two weeks, they had settled into a cool friendship. They joked with each other. They asked each other for advice. They laughed at the antics of the women.

Yes, she thought Kade Strong was hotter than a dozen *Playgirl* centerfolds combined—she could admit that—but the last thing she wanted was to get involved with a man who was so deeply in love with his dead wife. Besides, she enjoyed their newfound friendship, and after the Joaquin BS, she wasn't looking for love right now, anyway.

Kade Strong was her friend and nothing more. She was more than fine with that.

"Garcelle . . . Garcelle?"

She turned her head and focused her attention on her father, who was handing her the cordless phone. Did it ring? she wondered as she took the phone from him.

"Hel—"

"Garcelle, this is Kade. You're on a speaker-phone, okay?"

Garcelle placed her fork on her plate as she sat back from the table a bit. She furrowed her brow. "Okay," she said, with obvious hesitation.

"Long story short. I fell off a horse during a race—"

"You fell?" she shrieked. "Are you okay?"

"I'm fine. I'm more than fine. That's my whole point."

"You call breaking two ribs fine?" Garcelle heard a woman say in the background.

"You broke your ribs?" Garcelle gasped in horror.

"What is going on, Garcelle?" her father demanded in Spanish.

"Kade fell off a horse and broke his ribs," she told her father, holding the mouthpiece away from her mouth.

"I . . . didn't . . . break . . . anything," Kade roared into the phone. "I bruised my ribs."

"Oh, he *bruised* his ribs," Garcelle relayed to her father. She frowned as she focused again on the phone conversation. "And why were you horse racing at your age?"

"For the love of God, Garcelle—"

"Okay, okay. Go ahead." She placed the phone between her cheek and shoulder so that she could use both of her hands to twist her hair atop her head—a nervous gesture of hers.

"I know looking out for a grouchy injured man in his midthirties isn't a part of your baby-sitting duties, but I need a favor."

Garcelle rose from the table when she saw three sets of velvet brown eyes resting on her in open curiosity. "I'll do it," she said before he could even ask. She waved her hands to let her family know to continue with dinner. She left the kitchen, then walked through the living room and out the front door to sit down on the top step of the porch.

"Garcelle, are you sure? Because he could stay at Strong Ranch until he's better," Lisha Strong called out.

"It's no problem at all," she assured Kade's mother.

"Garcelle, I'm taking you off speakerphone, okay?" said Kade.

She heard the background noises disappear. "Kade, are you really okay? Just say yes or no."

"No. Hell, no," he said, with emphasis.

She bit back a smile. "It hurts like hell, doesn't it, Mr. Tough Guy?" she asked, her accent making *mister* sound more like *meester*.

He grunted. "Yes."

"When will you be home?" she asked as her eyes drifted up to watch the sun set.

"They're keeping me overnight to make sure I don't have a concussion."

Garcelle snorted in laughter. "For you to be horse racing, you had to have bumped your head *before* the race."

"Don't make me laugh, Garcelle," he said in a strained voice.

"You want me to come tonight?" she asked.

"No, don't bother. I'm about to run the whole Strong bunch out of here now." She heard protests in the background. "Kadina will spend tonight at my parents'."

"Well, I will pick you up from the hospital tomorrow," she told him as she rose from the step. She brushed any dust from her backside.

"You don't have to do that."

Garcelle shrugged as if he could see her. "Okay. I just thought I could get you and Kadina and take you home. That way we could part from your family at the hospital and not have to worry about clearing them out of your house."

The line went quiet for just a second. "Good idea," he said quickly. "I'll call you when I'm ready."

Garcelle laughed low and husky. "I thought so."

"Garcelle?"

"Yes, Kade?" she said as she walked back into the house.

"Thank you," he said warmly.

She ignored the shiver that raced down her spine and made her bare feet tingle. "*No problemo*. That's what friends are for."

5

Garcelle had just walked through the automatic doors of Colleton Medical Center when she spotted Rita and Pita climbing from their white station wagon. She didn't even break a sweat as she rode the elevator to the second floor of the three-story hospital. She smiled sweetly at the nurses at their station.

"Hello, I'm Kade Strong's sister," she lied, hoping none of the women knew the family and caught her. "Two women are on their way up to visit my brother, but we would like them barred from his room. Aggravation, you know?"

A petite blonde leaned forward in a conspiratorial fashion. "The women have been in and out of that room all morning. Even the hospital workers have been sniffing around like crazy. His room has got to be cleaner than an operating room."

Garcelle smiled.

"I must admit, he's not even my patient, and I've been in there *twice* to check on him," said the blond nurse.

"I'm glad you understand," Garcelle said, turning away from the station.

"Uh, why are you the only one with a Spanish accent?" the blond nurse called behind her.

Garcelle's steps slowed, and she turned. "I've been living in Mexico for a year. I guess you pick up more than just Montezuma's revenge."

She didn't give the woman a chance to say or ask anything else as she walked into Kade's room. Kadina jumped up from her seat by the bed and threw her arms around Garcelle's waist. Garcelle tugged on her ponytail playfully as she smiled in greeting at Kade's parents and then shifted her eyes to skim Kade's face.

He was sitting up on the side of the bed, in a black sweatsuit. His face was pensive but bruise free. "*Hola*, Kade Strong," she said softly.

Kade rose to his feet with effort. "Am I glad to see you," he said. "If I get one more flower or tin of cookies or pie or card or visit . . . I'm going to scream."

Garcelle looked around the room and thought she'd never seen so many flowers at a funeral. Some even lined the floor under his window. "Word sure travels fast," she said.

"Small-town living at its best," Kael said in that deep, gruff tone of his.

Garcelle sat down in the chair by Kade's bed. She looked up at him, with a huge grin. "What is it about you that's driving all these women crazy?" she asked in a low voice that was teasing and meant for his ears only.

"Don't see it, huh?" he asked as he pressed his hand to his side.

"You're all right," she said flippantly. "I've seen worse."

Kade laughed and then winced.

"Come on, Kadina. Let's all go see what snacks

they have downstairs in the café," Lisha said, rising and reaching her hand out to her granddaughter. Kael rose as well.

Kade looked over his shoulder at them. "Don't be long. The nurse said she'll be right back with my release papers."

They ignored him and filed right on out of the room.

Kade shook his head. "You know they left us alone on purpose," he told her.

"No," Garcelle said, with mock disbelief.

"As soon as they see a pretty face, they get to plotting."

Garcelle tilted her head to the side. "Ah. You think I'm pretty?" she asked, with saccharine sweetness.

Kade copied her arched eyebrow. "I've seen better."

"I don't get no complaints, baby," she told him, with Latin spice, before she rose from the chair and walked back over to the window.

"Do you have a boyfriend?" he asked suddenly.

"I used to," she said, looking out the window at the cars driving past the hospital. "It ended kind of bad, you know. So right now I'm just working to save for nursing school by baby-sitting this pretty little girl and playing bodyguard for her grouchy daddy."

Kade reached for one of his pillows and tossed it at her, with effort.

Lisha watched her granddaughter select and pay for a slice of chocolate cake. She thought of her son and Garcelle upstairs, and her eyes, which were so like Kade's, lit up.

"Uh oh," said Kael.

Lisha smoothed her hands over her jean slacks as she glanced over to her handsome husband. "What?" she asked, with mock innocence.

He shook his head. "Kade already told me that he and Garcelle are just friends, so just erase the thought from your mind."

"But didn't you see how comfortable they are with each other?" Lisha asked, lowering her voice as Kadina made her way across the café.

Kael's eyes rested on her. "Friends usually are comfortable with each other, Lisha."

She winked just like Kahron. "And sometimes friends become lovers," she whispered behind her hand as Kadina reached them.

A sharp dart of pain roused Kade from his nap. He winced as he smacked his mouth at the taste of sleep. It wasn't tasty.

Kade was propped up on pillows and in pajama bottoms. Both were a type of torture, because he loved sleeping on his stomach and in the nude. Releasing a deep breath, he turned his head on the pillow.

He hated being cooped up in his bedroom—this bedroom—all day. Everything about it reminded him of Reema. The brown, khaki, and gold décor. The wedding portrait on the wall. Even her perfume bottles still sat on the dresser top.

Since he'd moved back into the house, he'd purposely spent little time in the room. He left for work early and went to bed late. In the morning, he was dressed and out of the room in no time. At night he would shower and drop to sleep before he could even think about being in that room alone.

Now he was looking at at least three days of

relaxing for his ribs to heal, and there was *no* way he could spend it in this room. No way in hell.

He took his time flinging back the covers and sitting up on the side of the bed. He winced as a sharp pain vibrated across his side. "Damn," he swore.

"You are so damn hardheaded, Kade Strong."

He turned his head to find Garcelle leaning in the doorway and looking at him, with a chastising expression. "Leave me alone, Garcelle," he growled as he attempted to rise to his feet.

She rushed forward to help him, mumbling something in rapid Spanish under her breath.

"At least cuss me out in English," he grumbled as he rose to his feet.

Garcelle stood before him, with her hands on her deeply curved hips. "You get back in that bed, Kade Strong, or I will call your mama to come and get on your nerves while I go home."

He looked down into her vibrant eyes. "You do know that you work for me, and it's not the other way around," he snapped.

Garcelle licked her lips and looked down at the floor as she tapped her sandaled foot. She looked up at him, with a sigh. "What I do know is your mama's number."

Kade knew he had lost the battle. If he let his mother in his house, she would continue coming on the regular. He loved his mother, and he appreciated everything his parents did for him and Kadina after Reema died, but he needed his space. Giving Garcelle one last scowl, he eased back down onto the bed.

"Ha!" she said mockingly as she bent to position the covers over him.

"When this is over, I can fire you, you know," he told her.

Garcelle paused, with her body still bent over him and her nose just inches away from his. "I could quit *before* this is over, you know," she countered, her cool and fresh breath lightly fanning his mouth.

"You . . . " *Roses. She smells like roses.*

"Yes?" she asked, obviously awaiting his words.

Kade turned his head and looked at the adjoining bathroom. "Nothing. Never mind," he groused.

"*Perfecto,*" Garcelle said as she kicked off her shoes and walked around to the opposite side of the bed.

"Where's Kadina?" he asked, his eyes locked on her.

Garcelle reached in her back pocket for a deck of cards and flung it next to him on the bed. "She fell asleep watching *Maid in Manhattan.* We just love us some Jennifer Lopez."

"What are you doing?" Kade asked as he watched Garcelle climb onto the bed.

She froze, with one knee pressed into the thick and plush mattress, as she looked at him with a critical eye. "What do you *think* I'm doing, Kade Strong? I know you are not conceited enough to think I'm jumping in bed to have nookie with you."

"Of course not."

"Good." Garcelle carefully climbed on the bed, sat cross-legged, and then shuffled the deck of cards. "I know this room must be driving you crazy, so I'm here to keep you company until your brothers get here after work."

He had to admit that ever since she'd walked into the room, it hadn't felt quite so claustrophobic. "You know how to play whist?" he asked.

"No," she said, handing him the deck. "But teach me. I'm a quick learner."

"Learning how to play whist isn't that easy."

Garcelle shrugged. "My ex told me the same thing about poker, and now he can hardly beat me."

Kade was surprised. "You play poker?"

Garcelle lifted a brow. "A little something," she said, with a saucy grin and a wink.

Bianca washed her hands at the small sink in the tack room of the barn. She dried her hands with disposable towels as she walked out of the metal building. Her full and pouty lips curled into a soft smile as she read the sign on the door:

KING EQUINE SERVICES /
BIANCA KING VETERINARY CLINIC
A FULL-SERVICE EQUINE FARM

So far every decision she'd made concerning her business, her family, and her love life had been a good one. The equine veterinary practice, which she'd opened right on her father's horse farm, was already thriving and showing a profit. That was mainly because more than a few of her clients from her old Atlanta practice would drive the distance to South Carolina or had highly recommended her to local farmers. The small metal building she erected on the east portion of the property was smaller than her old practice, but she was pleased with the setup and with the fact that she was still able to work with her father daily.

She had had to travel back to Holtsville to snatch the family business from ruin because of her father's alcoholism, but every bit of the success was now his doing. He had been sober for over a year. His divorce to his treacherous wife was finalized. He was in full control of the business and was delivering that special Hank King touch with the horses.

And Kahron. Bianca moaned a bit in pleasure as she thought of her love for her husband. He had once asked her to trust him, and when she finally did give in, she found a love that plenty of folks would give their right hand for.

In fact, she was headed home early for the first time in weeks so that she could spend some quality time with her man. She would warm up one of Garcelle's frozen dinners, take a hot bath, slip into something that was barely there and wait for Kahron to walk through the door for a helluva surprise.

"Headed home?"

Bianca turned to find her father, a tall, big, barrel-shaped man, walking up behind her. She slowed to a stop and threw her arm around his waist when he caught up to her.

"Yes. Yes. Yes," she said, with emphasis.

He laughed, and his laughter rumbled like a thunderstorm in his chest. "You and Kahron have a special night planned?"

"I'm gonna try my best," she said as they neared the front porch of her father's home.

"Good. Because I have some plans of my own for the weekend," he said, with a chuckle that was decidedly boyish.

"Who?" she asked, surprised. Bianca hadn't even known her father was dating anyone.

"An out-of-town guest," he admitted as they climbed the stairs together.

"Do I know—"

Honk-honk.

Bianca's curly head whipped around and her eyes widened as a gold convertible Jaguar came barreling toward the house. It lurched to a stop just in time to miss hitting the front porch.

"Surprise, surprise, sweetie!"

Bianca forced a smile to her face. "Mimi?" she said, watching as the petite spitfire hopped out of the car in a getup that could only be called urban cowgirl. A jean pantsuit, cowboy hat, and a belt buckle large enough to knock a bull unconscious.

"My daddy's . . . dating . . . *Mimi,*" Bianca said in a confused voice before her older friend enveloped her in a hug that was all Chanel parfum.

Garcelle and Kadina were in the kitchen, making Kade's favorite double chocolate and walnut brownies. Kadina wanted to do something special for her father, and Garcelle knew he could use a treat after the spanking she'd given him in poker earlier that day. Thank God they'd played for Monopoly money and not clothes, because Kade Strong would have been as naked as the day he was born.

Not that she wanted to see Kade nude.

Garcelle's eyebrow rose and her lips pursed as she envisioned Kade naked and bronzed, with his muscles oiled and well defined. She already knew from seeing him without his shirt that the man's body was sculptured from his long hours of farmwork. He had just the right amount of fine silver hair on his chest. Just enough for a woman to play in as she lay in bed with him.

Garcelle looked down into the bowl of chocolate, and she bit her bottom lip as she clearly pictured herself nude and riding Kade, astride a galloping horse and through a field of flowers. As he rode the horse faster and faster, she rode him harder and harder. Each movement of the horse's hindquarters sent his shaft deeper inside of her as she held on to him for dear life.

Was it possible to ride a man while riding a horse?

The doorbell rang, and Garcelle frowned as the image faded away in her mind. Having a freaky daydream about Kade Strong was just plain *stupido*, and having a freaky daydream about being on a horse with Kade Strong was ridiculous, because she didn't fool with horses at all.

"I'll get it," Kadina said, jumping down off the stool and running out of the kitchen.

Garcelle was spreading the brownie mix into the glass bakeware when she heard Kadina say, "My daddy's sleeping. He don't need no prayer."

Garcelle grabbed the dish towel to clean her hands as she made her way out of the kitchen to the front door. She rolled her eyes heavenward at the woman standing there, holding a bible, but dang near dressed for the club. "Can I help you?" Garcelle asked as she pulled Kadina behind her.

The woman looked Garcelle up and down with a slow thoroughness before she visibly stiffened her spine. "And you are?" she asked, with attitude.

Oh no, she didn't, Garcelle thought, with sistahgirl spunk. "I'm Garcelle Santos, Kadina's *niñera*. Can I help you?"

"A nina what?" the woman asked.

"She's my nanny," Kadina said, moving forward to stand beside Garcelle.

"Oh . . . okay then," the woman said, with a big, cheesy grin. "My name is Portia Klinton. I attend church with Kade. Could you let him know I'm here to check on him?"

It was Garcelle's turn to take in the woman's skintight pants and formfitting T-shirt. "Listen, he's asleep. I'll let him know you dropped by."

She started to close the door, but Portia put her foot in the doorway. Garcelle backed up, opened the door wide, and looked at the woman like she was crazy.

Portia went in her bag and pulled out a small pad and pen. "If you're not too busy to take a message?" she said, with false sweetness.

Garcelle held her hand out. "Of course not," she said, with mock sincerity.

Portia pressed the note into Garcelle's hand. Garcelle looked down and immediately recognized both the handwriting and the phone number. It was 555-0000. The woman was the freaky secret admirer. Since that first grotesque dildo, the woman had sent Kade eight other gifts, each more sexually explicit than the last.

"I'll make sure it's properly delivered," Garcelle said, with her heavy accent.

"Please do," said Portia.

"You know, I've been watching reruns of this show called *Martin*," Garcelle told Portia.

"And?" Portia retorted, with attitude.

"I learned something that I want to show you."

Portia looked confused.

"Step back a little," Garcelle said in a friendly tone.

Portia took a step back. "Now what?"

Garcelle tilted her head to the side. "This," she said sweetly before she stepped back and swung the door closed.

"Now to make sure it's properly delivered, the way I promised," Garcelle said over her shoulder to Kadina as she strolled back into the kitchen. She balled up the paper and threw it up into the air like she was making a free throw. It landed in the trash, with a swoosh.

Kadina covered her mouth with both of her hands as she burst into a fit of giggles.

6

Garcelle tossed and turned in her bed. She flipped from her back onto her stomach and onto her back again. Her smoky brown eyes opened, and she turned her head on the pillow to look at her night-stand clock. 12:15 a.m.

She couldn't sleep.

She pulled back her curtain and looked up at the night sky. The moon was completely full and seemed close enough to touch. It was beautiful and haunting all at once.

Kicking back the covers, Garcelle hopped out of bed in her wifebeater and an old pair of men's boxers. She padded barefoot to the kitchen and headed straight to the fridge for a can of light beer. She popped the tab and took a deep gulp.

"It's a little late for that, isn't it?"

Gabrielle nearly choked on the beer as she whirled around and found her father sitting at the kitchen table, cloaked by darkness. "Papi, what are you doing up?" she asked as she reached over to the wall to turn on the light.

"I sit here sometimes and look at your mother's

picture as the moonlight comes through the door."
Carlos leaned forward and pushed back the chair
at the head of the table. "Bring me one," he told
her in Spanish.

Garcelle grabbed another beer before she walked
across the small kitchen to take the seat. She passed
him the beer before she took another sip of her
own. "Papi, you know we wouldn't be upset if you
wanted to start dating again," she told him. She hes-
itated before she said the rest. "I don't think Mami
would mind, either."

Carlos took a long swig of his beer before he
looked over at his daughter, with his boyishly handsome face. "When you love somebody the way that
I loved my Maria and you lose them, your heart is
so tied up with trying to heal. You feel like a piece
of you—a big piece of you—is gone. So your heart
doesn't have room to fill it with love for someone
else. It wouldn't be fair to that person. Until the
heart heals, you would forever make comparisons.
It takes time."

Garcelle used her fingertip to trace the top of the
can as she fell silent. She was up at midnight, sipping
beer while she talked to her father, because she
couldn't sleep. And she couldn't sleep, because with
each passing day, her physical attraction to Kade
Strong was growing. The man *was* gorgeous. Tempt-
ingly delicious. Devilishly handsome. Devastatingly
sexy. Disarmingly charming. Distractingly appealing.

She was a healthy, red-blooded woman, with a
healthy libido, *when* she allowed that door to be
opened . . . but she didn't want to be attracted to
Kade Strong. She didn't want to keep dreaming of
making wild and kinky love to him astride a horse.
She didn't want to go to sleep and dream of his

hands and mouth and tongue . . . and other things pleasing to her. She didn't want to wake up to find that just a dream of that man had the bud between her legs visibly pulsating. A wet dream!

Garcelle released a heavy breath.

"Something you want to talk about?" Carlos asked as he rose to pour the rest of his beer down the drain.

She shook her head and took another sip of her beer. His words of undying and unending love for his wife were proof positive that Kade Strong, the handsome and oh so sexy grieving widower, was not a man to even consider catching feelings about. During the last few weeks, they had settled into a platonic friendship that she enjoyed.

He was her friend, and that was all they would be. That was all she wanted them to be. Period.

Carlos tugged on Garcelle's ponytail as he walked out of the kitchen. "Go to bed," he told her, with a yawn.

She drained the last of her beer and then tossed the can into the trash. "Papi, anyone ever tell you that you look like Oscar de La Hoya?" she asked.

Carlos laughed richly and fully as he reached his bedroom door. "That's the beer talking. Good night, Garcelle."

She walked into her bedroom and closed the door behind her before she climbed into bed. Perhaps the beer would put her to sleep so deeply that she wouldn't even dream of Kade Strong.

Kadina climbed out of her bed and made her way across the cool hardwood floor to the pastel-colored curio cabinet in the corner of her room.

Her father had said that before she was born, her
mother had picked out each and every one of the
glass and crystal figurines in the cabinet. Kadina
carefully opened the glass door and stood up on
her toes to flick a switch in the cabinet. A small
light popped on, and a sweet lullaby, like in a music
box, began to play.

She closed the cabinet door, with a small *click*,
and stepped back to enjoy the way the figurines
seemed to sparkle in the darkness as the music
played. She smiled before she climbed back in bed
and got under the covers. She turned on her side
so that she could look at the curio cabinet from
where she lay.

She hadn't told a soul that one night last week,
she'd dreamt that she was just a baby in her mother's
arms in front of the lit curio cabinet as her mother
sung her that same lullaby. It had seemed so real. For
the first time in a long time, she'd felt a connection
to her mother.

Whenever she couldn't sleep or her new room
was just too much for her, she would turn on the
curio cabinet and feel her mother's presence there
in the room, watching over her.

It wasn't long at all before her eyes drifted closed
and she felt the wind coming through the window
touch her cheek like a kiss.

Hank kissed the top of Mimi's head, which rested
on his chest. It felt good to have her warm body
snuggled close to his. Damn good.

Who knew that his daughter's eccentric friend
would turn out to be just what he needed when he
needed it. A dance at Bianca and Kahron's wedding

had turned into nearly six months of phone conversations. Bianca didn't even know that he'd been down to Atlanta twice to spend the weekend with Mimi.

She was good for him. He could tell her anything. Ask her anything. And it wasn't Mimi in her "I'm wild, and I'll say anything to get attention" mode. She was calm, laid back, rational, logical, and smart. This was Beulah.

He chuckled to think he was probably the only person alive who knew that was her real name. She swore she'd gut him with a fork if he told a soul.

He loved her, and she loved him. They had decided it was time for Bianca to know, and so this time Mimi had come to him. They hadn't wanted to spring it on her like they did, but who knew Bianca would be standing there the exact moment Mimi arrived. The look on Bianca's face had been priceless.

Honestly, he couldn't tell if she was pleased or not, but it didn't matter. After the hell Trishon had put him through, his daughter should be happy for him.

Mimi stirred in her sleep. She smacked her lips slightly as she tilted her head up to look at him in the moonlight. Her hair was wild and mussed. Her make-up was gone, except for those long eyelashes. The scent of her perfume mingled with the scent of the sex. She had never looked or smelled better to him.

"Hey, you," she said, her voice more husky and soft.

His grin widened as he felt her hand firmly close around his growing erection. "Say it for me," he pleaded as she placed her nude and svelte body atop his.

Mimi rolled her eyes heavenward. "Do I have to?" she asked in her natural voice.

"Please."

She cleared her throat and swallowed hard. "You and me makes we," she said in the mock nasal tone of hers.

They laughed together until Mimi straddled his hips and proved to him that at *that* moment, there wasn't a darn thing funny.

Bianca tightly grasped Kahron's buttocks as he stroked deeply within her. Each stroke brought a gasp from deep within her until she felt she'd go breathless. As they came to a spasmodic climax together, she kissed his shoulder and then his neck.

Kahron rolled over onto his back, bringing her body atop his as he remained planted within her until his hardness eased. He stroked her back. "You okay?" he asked.

Bianca lifted her head from his sweaty chest to look at him. "Wasn't it as good as always?" she whispered to him in the moonlight.

"Actually . . ."

Bianca's mouth dropped open in surprise and a bit of hurt. "Actually what?" she snapped.

"Physically everything was as good as always, but as much as I know I put it down—and I did lay it on you—I could tell you weren't all there. It's like your mind was somewhere else."

Bianca kissed his chin, enjoying the feel of his stubble against her lips. "You're right. I wasn't all there. I'm sorry, baby."

"Wanna talk about it?"

Bianca rolled off of him and then sat on the edge of the bed, with her legs crossed. She grabbed a pillow and held it close in front of her. "I love my father, and I want him to be happy. And I love Mimi to death. . . ."

"But," Kahron urged as he rolled over onto his side to lightly massage her lower back.

"*But* I would rather get into the ring with barbeque sauce on my ears and fight Mike Tyson."

Kahron laughed. "Day-um, is it like *that*?" he asked.

Bianca turned to him, with a serious look on her face. "Oh, it's like that."

"Because . . ."

"Because Mimi is a drunk. She sips on liquor all day long from her flask like it's water. She may not act like a drunk. She may not talk like she's drunk or smell like she's drunk, but trust me, her ass be drunk."

"So you're worried your dad will fall off the wagon?"

Bianca flung her hands in the air, knocking the pillow to the floor. "Off the wagon? Shit. I'm scared she's gone drag him under the wheels of the wagon."

"Talk to your dad. Let him know how you feel. Hell, be honest with Mimi, too."

Bianca nodded as she dropped her chin into her hand. "He's just worked really hard to get himself together, and I'd hate for it all to go to waste. His life, his business. Us."

Kahron flung back the covers, sat up, and moved behind his wife. He wrapped his legs and arms around her and kissed the sweet hollow of her neck.

At that moment—at least for that moment—in her husband's arms, Bianca felt at peace.

* * *

The hooves of the horse pounded the dirt as Kade rode as if the fiery doors of hell were singeing his heels. The sun was blazing down on his back as he rode the endless stretch of emerald green grass. He rode effortlessly to the top of the hill. The muscles in his arms tensed as he used the reins to bring the horse to a halt.

Kade looked down at the valley below him. It was as beautiful as the Garden of Eden. The sounds of nature surrounded him. His eyes honed in on the crystal blue lake just as a figure appeared from beneath the depths. Even from a distance, he could tell the figure was that of a sultry and seductive woman, whose curves defied reality as gravity pulled the water from her body. Droplets raced across her caramel skin to pause at the tips of her nipples before they fell from her body.

Here, in this picturesque setting, he was the Adam to her Eve, and this was the perfect spot to give in to temptation.

He quickly stripped off his clothing, freeing his throbbing erection, before he kicked the horse's sides and went racing down the hill at a thunderous pace. She looked up as he neared her, but she barely had time to blink as he bent over and scooped her body up with one strong arm. With ease, he brought her up onto the saddle, facing him.

Her arms and legs surrounded him as she blessed him with a dozen tiny kisses from one broad shoulder to the next. As he focused his eyes ahead and controlled the horse's gallop with one strong hand, Kade wrapped his free arm around her waist and pulled her higher up on his lap until the lips of her thick and moist core cupped his shaft. He brought the horse to a stop in the middle of a field of colorful wildflowers. His Eve leaned backward, with her breasts pushed forward, taunting him. With a low growl, he buried his head in her sweet cleavage, leaving kisses on each bronzed globe before he shifted to capture one throbbing hard nipple in his mouth.

"Ah," she cried out as her fingernails began digging into the strong muscles of his shoulders.

He circled the nipple with his moist tongue before he blew cool air on it, causing her to shiver uncontrollably in his arms. On to the next nipple. He repeated the delicious move. She shivered again.

"Oh, Garcelle," he moaned against her flesh.

His head jerked up, and he looked down into her face. That beautiful face, with wide, doe-like eyes that haunted him. Teased him. Caressed him. Drew him in.

Garcelle was his Eve. His temptress. His temptation.

He locked his eyes with hers as she slowly sat up to face him. "You want this as much as I do, don't you, Kade?" she asked in Spanish.

"Yes," he submitted. "Yes."

The first taste of her lips made him harder. He felt his thighs quivering from a need to be deeply buried inside of her warmth. As she deepened the kiss with the hotness of her tongue, Kade tightened his hold around her waist, lifted her up with ease, and then guided her back down onto his hardness.

Their mouths opened as they both gasped. Their chests heaved, and their breathing was shaky. Their hearts pounded.

He captured her lips for a quick kiss before he buried his face against her chest as she began to move her hips against him. Each move gripped and then released his shaft with slick ease. He closed his eyes tightly and fought for control as she lowered her head and whispered hotly in his ear in Spanish as she rode him.

"¿Es bueno?"

"Yes, it's damn good," he answered, with a moan, against the plushness of her breast.

She licked his ear lobe as she moved her hips to the left.

"¿Quisieras que parara?"

He shook his head as his hand massaged her buttocks. "No, I don't want you to stop."

She laughed huskily as she moved her wide hips to the right.

"Dicen que soy la mejor," she said.

Kade leaned back and looked in her sultry eyes. "Damn right, you're the best."

She kissed him as she swiveled her hips 360 delicious degrees.

Kade felt a fine sheen of sweat coat his muscles as he clenched his teeth, fighting so that he wouldn't explode deep within her.

He kicked the horse's flanks, causing it to move forward at a slow and easy trot through the field. The movement of the horse caused their bodies to jostle, sending his shaft deeper against her walls.

His hands tightly grasped her soft buttocks as she clasped her hands behind his neck and leaned backward. The horse's trot caused her full breasts to rise and fall against her chest as her hair blew in the wind, mingling with the horse's flying mane.

Never had he seen a more glorious sight.

His blood surged through him, hardening him until he ached. "Make me come, Garcelle," he moaned as he watched her with intense eyes.

"Make me come . . . Make me come . . . Make me come . . . ," Kade murmured as his hands rose in the darkness of night. His fingers were cupped as his hips rose slightly off the bed, and he felt like his seed was going to spill. "Make me come, Garcelle."

Kade's eyes shot open, and he sat up in bed. He hollered out hoarsely at the pain that raced across his ribs. Sweat coated his body. His heart raced. His loins ached. His penis was as hard as stone between his legs and tenting the sweat-soaked sheets.

He winced as he remembered every erotic detail of his dream. What the hell was going on with him?

He wanted Garcelle . . . badly. But it couldn't be. It wouldn't be. He was not ready. He felt guilty about dreaming of another woman in the bed he had once shared with his wife.

Yes, Garcelle was beautiful. Garcelle was smart. Garcelle had a body that could stop traffic on Highway 17 in *both* directions. He was a man. A man with good vision and great blood flow.

Oh God, was she woman. All woman.

But this could not happen. It would not happen. He would make sure of that.

7

"Go fish, Daddy," Kadina said, with a chuckle, as she fell backwards on the floor.

Garcelle plucked a card from the deck and handed it to him so that he didn't have to reach from his spot on the couch, where he was lounging. Their hands briefly touched, and the card drifted to the floor as they both pulled away as if they'd been shocked.

"Excuse me," Garcelle said.

"No, I'm sorry," Kade said.

Garcelle reached for the card and handed it to him. She looked up at Kadina and found the little girl looking at them, with a scrunched-up face.

"What's wrong with y'all?" Kadina asked, her Southern accent sounding almost like a Texas twang.

Garcelle and Kade looked at each other and then looked away. "Nothing," they quickly said in unison before glancing at each other again.

"Okay," Kadina said simply, with a shrug, before she focused on the cards in her hand. "Garcelle, do you have a . . . three?"

Garcelle folded her legs where she sat on the

floor. She shook her head. "Kadina, go fish, sweetheart, and then let me have those deuces."

"Aw, man," Kadina whined as she handed the card to Garcelle.

"Boy, I am so good at this game," Garcelle teased them as she laid down her pair.

"You do learn card games fast," Kade said dryly as he shifted his cards in his hand.

Garcelle winked at him as she playfully tossed her hair over her shoulder. "*No odies al jugador; odia el juego.*"

Kade smiled at her. "Could you talk crap to me in English, please?"

Kadina giggled. "It means, 'Don't hate the player; hate the game,' Daddy."

"Oh God, am I going to have both of you around here speaking Spanish?"

"*Sí, Papi,*" Garcelle and Kadina both said. They looked at each other and laughed before they gave each other a high five.

"Lord, help me," Kade drawled as he watched them.

They continued to play, and although Garcelle had learned the child's card game quickly, Kadina was the true master, and she beat them twice. As they dealt a new hand, Garcelle bit her thumbnail and glanced over at Kade as he lounged in old Dickies pants and a T-shirt, with a pair of ratty slippers that had seen better days.

At that moment she was aware of her attraction to Kade, but it wasn't her focus. She was just enjoying being in his and Kadina's company. They were friends. That was it. She felt so much better than she had last night around twelve, when she woke up in a sweat, with thoughts of stallions—

and riding the two-legged variety atop the four-legged one.

Don't even go there, Garcelle. No way. No how.

The doorbell rang, and Garcelle jumped to her feet, more than glad for the diversion from her thoughts. "I'll get it," she said over her shoulder as she left the den.

She smoothed her hands over her I'M TOO HOT FOR YOU T-shirt and sweatpants. The front door was open, but the glass screen door was locked, so Garcelle was able to see the unfamiliar woman standing there. *"Otro cazador de hombre. La pena buena,"* she muttered under her breath, with a suck of her teeth, thinking it was indeed another of the man chasers wanting to put their hooks in Kade.

Although, Garcelle had to admit that this one was trying another approach. Her hair was pulled into a professional topknot, the make-up on her face was minimal, and her jeans slacks and buttoned-up pinstripe shirt were a definite change from the hotties who rolled through in clothes tight enough to spark a fire from friction.

She noticed the woman's eyes widen and then damn near close as she squinted at the sight of her.

Garcelle unlocked the door and put on a smile. "Hello. Can I help you?" she said, with plenty of pleasantness.

"Oh . . . you're Spanish?" the woman said in a whisper, her soft voice filled with surprise. "You don't look it."

Garcelle's spine stiffened, and she had to swallow her irritation, because this was not her house and this woman was not her guest. Ignoring the woman's rudeness, she said, "Can I help you?"

"Well, I thought this home was still owned by

Kade Strong, but I guess I'm wrong," she said, looking up at Garcelle.

"This is Kade Strong's house. Can I help you?"

"I'm Zorrie . . . Zorrie Kintrell. I'm a friend of the family."

"Aunt Zorrie?" Kadina called from the den. Seconds later there were running footsteps. Kadina appeared at the door in no time and flung herself at the woman, wrapping her long, skinny arms around her waist.

Zorrie bent over a bit to hug her back. "Kadina? Oh, you've gotten so big. Step back, and let me see you, sweetheart."

Garcelle smiled at the obvious pleasure on Kadina's face. "Hello, Zorrie. I'm Kadina's nanny, Garcelle," she said, offering the woman her hand.

Zorrie took her offered hand warmly. "Nice to meet you. I'm Reema's best friend."

"Come in, of course," said Garcelle. She stepped back and watched as Kadina pulled the woman into the den. Garcelle closed the door and moved into the kitchen to leave them alone with their guest.

She glanced at the clock. It was a little after two in the afternoon, and in the Spanish culture, it was time for *la comida*, or lunch. Since it was Kade's first full day at home recuperating from his injuries, she decided to make the traditional heavy meal. As she listened to the laughter floating from the den, Garcelle focused on preparing a multicourse meal of vegetable soup, stuffed cod with fried potatoes and sautéed green beans on the side, and for dessert, a *compota de peras*, or pear compote.

Since their move to America, and especially since Maria Santos's passing, the Santos family had gotten away from the tradition. It felt good to do something that put her in touch with her culture. It took a solid thirty minutes, but in the end, Garcelle knew she made a fabulous meal.

Garcelle wiped her hands on a dish towel as she made her way to the den. She paused in the doorway. Zorrie was sitting on the edge of couch, beside Kade's legs, and Kadina was on the floor, on her knees, as they all looked at a photo album. Zorrie reached out and touched Kade's arm as they laughed together at something Kadina said about a photo of her mother.

"Something smells delicious," Zorrie said.

"I made a traditional Spanish lunch," Garcelle said, walking into the room.

"Thanks, Garcelle. 'Cause I am starving," Kade said as he looked up at her.

His eyes were the brightest and most alive she had ever seen them. Was it the photos or the presence of Zorrie?

"Aunt Zorrie, you have to stay for lunch. Garcelle is the best cook ever," Kadina said as she rose to her feet.

"Well, don't forget your mother could throw down in the kitchen, too," Zorrie said as she rose.

"Kade, can you make it to the kitchen, or do you want me to bring you a tray?" Garcelle asked.

Kade swung his legs to the floor and eased his way to the end of the couch. "You tightened these bandages real good for me this morning, so I'm going to the table."

Garcelle stepped forward to offer Kade some assistance, but Zorrie got to him before her. Her instant reaction was to feel slighted, but she decided that that was being childish.

"*Bueno*, Daddy," Kadina said, with her eyes on him as he rose gingerly to his feet.

"Oh . . . your nanny is teaching you Spanish?" Zorrie asked as they made their way to the kitchen.

Garcelle thought she heard a hint of derision beneath Zorrie's sugary sweet tone.

"*Sí*," Kadina said, with a wink at Garcelle.

Garcelle tugged Kadina's ponytail.

"Garcelle is good for Kadina. I'm lucky she was able to help me out this summer," Kade said as he took a seat at the large island in the center of the brightly lit room.

"Yes, of course," replied Zorrie.

Garcelle moved to the stove to begin serving the first course of soup. She had to swallow her uneasiness at serving Zorrie. It made her feel like the maid she wasn't. When it was the three of them, everything was informal, like a favor between friends.

"And I can't wait to spend some time with my godchild. Work has kept me from visiting South Carolina more often," Zorrie said, with a warm smile at Kadina. "I think it's been a year, and even then, I was just in town for a funeral, and I went right back that same weekend. We had fun that weekend, too. Remember we went to the museum in Charleston?"

Garcelle served herself a bowl of soup and sat at the island, beside Kadina. Her spine stiffened when Zorrie reacted to her presence at the table with obvious surprise and disapproval.

Garcelle just smiled around her spoonful of soup. She wished Kade would tell her she wasn't allowed to eat with the family. She *wished* he would.

Kade reached for a piece of bread at the same time as Garcelle. They both pulled their hands back.

"So how long are you in town for, Zorrie?" Kade asked as he broke off a piece of bread.

Good question.

"Two, maybe three, weeks," Zorrie said, with a long stare at Garcelle, which Garcelle met boldly.

Kadina jumped up and down in her seat excitedly. "Aunt Zorrie, you have to spend a couple of nights with me. Please."

"I would love to, but it's up to your daddy," said Zorrie.

"Fine with me," he said, digging into his soup with gusto.

Garcelle completely lost her appetite.

Bianca was staring out her office window at the ranch hands working the Travises' new racehorse, Shogun. It was a slow day at the clinic, and she wished it were otherwise. She wanted nothing more than to have something on her mind besides her father and Mimi's relationship.

What . . . the . . . hell?

She was grinning and bearing it all, but deep down, she wanted to flip out and ask them both if they were crazy. It was building up inside of her with every passing moment. She was sick of the questions flying in and out of her head at any odd moment of the day. And her main question was, When did their love affair begin?

Her office door opened, and Bianca turned away from the window to find her father and Mimi walking into her office, arm in arm. She rolled her eyes before she could catch herself.

"You busy, Bunny?" her father asked as he looked down at her.

Bianca cleared her throat and began to shuffle papers on her desk. "Actually, I'm swamped," she lied, looking at them briefly, with a stiff smile, before she focused her full attention on the papers.

"Something wrong, sweetie?" Mimi asked as she stepped forward in a pink suit with enough fringes to offend a cowboy.

Bianca looked up at her briefly. "No, not at all. What are you two up to today?"

Mimi slid her petite frame on the corner of Bianca's desk and crossed her legs. Her gold heels were covered with the dust of the farm. "I was telling Big Daddy—"

"Big . . . Daddy?" Bianca asked, with a hint of derision.

Mimi smiled like a cat before a bowl of cream. "He's your daddy, sweetie, but he's my, huh, what . . . Big Daddy. That's right."

Hank's smile was big enough to show every tooth in his head.

"Anyway, I was telling Big Daddy that I want to experience a big old country barbeque with all the works," said Mimi. "I want to try all those things Big Daddy has been telling me about. Venison, coon, catfish stew, and . . . and . . ."

"Frogmaw stew," Hank offered.

Mimi clapped her bejeweled hands. "Yes, that's it. Frogmaw stew that *isn't* made with frogs, right? A lady has to draw the line somewhere."

Bianca laughed at her friend. In that moment she realized that she'd been so busy pouting over their relationship that she hadn't allowed herself to enjoy having Mimi around.

"You and Kahron be sure to come Saturday, and tell the rest of that big ole Strong bunch," Hank said as he walked over to massage Mimi's shoulder as he kissed her forehead.

Mimi wore enough make-up to make a man look like a woman, and Bianca was surprised her father's lips weren't covered with foundation.

"Me and a couple of the hands are headed to Charleston," Hank added. "You two enjoy your day together."

Bianca felt alarmed. She wasn't ready to be alone with Mimi. All her feelings about their relationship might explode out of her like confetti.

"I told Big Daddy that I'd stay here with you. It's not good to crowd a man," Mimi said, patting her jet-black French roll in a bad Mae West imitation.

Bianca genuinely smiled up at her.

"I can help with those horses, honey," said Mimi.

Bianca leaned back in her chair. "There aren't any . . . ahem . . . male horses to take a peek at," she teased.

Mimi hopped off the desk and wrapped her arms around Hank's wide girth. "I have my own stallion to show me a big and hard—"

"Ick alert! Ick alert!" Bianca yelled, not caring how childish it was for her to cover her ears with her hands.

Hank picked Mimi up, bringing her face closer to his. They kissed long and firm, like they were in the room alone.

"Daughter in the room," Bianca said, with emphasis.

Mimi flung her head back as she lifted one hand and used her thumb to wipe her crimson red lipstick from Hank's thick lips. "I'm sorry, sweetie," she said in the caricature voice of hers as she stared dreamily into Hank's eyes. "When I'm around Big Daddy, he just makes me . . . *come* alive."

They laughed while Bianca dropped her head into her hands. "Good grief," she muttered.

8

By the time Friday rolled around, Garcelle was ready to kick her size eight feet at Zorrie's picture-perfect, phony behind. The woman was driving her *muy loca*, hanging around the house so much. With Kade having returned to work, he wasn't there to act as a buffer. Garcelle's nerves were seriously grated. Seriously.

The woman had an opinion—whether spoken or not—about everything. If she had to stand Zorrie hovering over her shoulder while she cooked a meal, she was going to tie her behind up like a turkey. And whenever Kadina showed Garcelle too much affection or attention, Zorrie was there to bring up Reema, as if Garcelle was trying to take her place.

How ridiculous, considering Garcelle was probably one of the few single women in Holtsville respecting Kade's grief.

The sun was on the rise, and the skies were becoming a deep shade of purple and lavender, as Garcelle parked her Cabrio in front of Kade's house. For the first time since she'd taken the job as

Kadina's caregiver, Garcelle was dreading going to work. She uttered some less than friendly terms for Zorrie Kintrell as she eyed the woman's white Mercedes Benz, which was parked beside Kade's SUV.

Zorrie must have spent the night. For one foolish moment, Garcelle wondered where she slept, and a jealousy like nothing she had ever known consumed her as she envisioned Kade making love to the woman. But Kade wouldn't sleep with his dead wife's best friend in the very house he'd shared with his wife. *That* Garcelle knew for sure.

She climbed out of the car and grabbed the small bag of groceries. She'd brought the ingredients to make *churros* for breakfast. She knew that Kadina loved the sweet fried dough. That, plus some hot chocolate, would start their day off just right.

Garcelle walked up to the front door just as it swung open. Kade came barreling out. They collided. Garcelle went flying backwards, landing on her back, with a grunt of pain. The groceries rolled out of the bag and scattered across the porch.

"Garcelle? Are you okay?" Kade asked, his mint-fresh breath lightly caressing her face as he knelt beside her. He pressed his palm to her cheek, and Garcelle gasped at the hot jolt of electricity that went through her from his simple touch.

"I'm fine, even though you're a big wall of muscle to run into," she quipped as she sat up. "Are your ribs okay?"

Kade nodded as he rose to his feet and offered her his hand. "Don't worry about me. I'm a grown-ass man."

Yes, you are, she thought as she slipped her hand into his.

He pulled her to her feet, and then Garcelle

stumbled forward, causing their bodies to press to-gether, with their clutched hands between them.

Garcelle looked up at Kade. Kade looked down at Garcelle. She released a shaky breath as her heart pounded wildly. He licked his mouth as his intense eyes dropped down to her open mouth. She licked her own lips and then bit her bottom lip nervously.

"Garcelle," he said huskily as he lifted his free hand to caress the side of her face.

She leaned into his touch as she inhaled lightly.

Pure electricity and fire crackled around them as they stood there, absorbing each other. Heat pressed between their bodies. Their hearts roared like thunder. The chemistry between them was explosive and hot . . . like fire.

"Damn, Garcelle," he said again, his voice and his eyes so obviously tortured.

She saw that he struggled with his desire for her, and it tore at her heart. As badly as she wanted to feel his lips pressed on hers, Garcelle allowed her-self one last look of longing at his mouth before she looked up in his eyes. "You're not ready for this, Kade," she told him huskily. "We both know you're not ready."

He nodded as he caressed her bottom lip with his thumb.

Garcelle turned her face and pressed her lips to his palm. "*Podría enamorarme de ti muy, muy facil-mente,*" she whispered before she stepped back from him and awkwardly put her groceries into the bag.

Kade reached out and grabbed her arm. "Gar-celle, I—"

"Kade?"

Garcelle looked past him and saw Zorrie standing

in the doorway, in a knee-length satin robe. Kade released Garcelle with obvious regret as Zorrie stepped out onto the porch to stand beside him.

Kade headed down the stairs. "Good-bye, ladies," he flung over his broad shoulder as he jogged down the stairs.

"Garcelle, why are you here today?" Zorrie asked as if she was her employer and not Kade.

Garcelle gazed at the other woman. "Excuse me?"

Kade swore before he turned on the bottom step. "Garcelle, I meant to call you this morning before you left home. Zorrie's going to spend a couple of days here with Kadina, so you can have the weekend off . . . with pay, of course."

Garcelle hoisted her bag into her arms. "Thanks, Kade," she said as she gave Zorrie one last irritated look before she jogged down the steps as well.

"No problem," he replied.

As she passed Kade, who was climbing into his vehicle, they glanced at one another and then quickly glanced away.

"Bye, Kade. Have a good day at work," Zorrie called from the porch, like a wife seeing her husband off for the day.

He just waved before he reversed out of the yard ahead of Garcelle.

As she drove away from the house, Garcelle frowned in thought. At first she'd thought Zorrie was hanging around to protect the interest of her deceased friend; now Garcelle thought the woman was nothing but another man hunter in disguise.

Zorrie watched Garcelle reverse her beat-up little Volkswagen out of the yard. With each turn of the wheels carrying Garcelle farther from the house, Zorrie's face changed, losing its pleasantness. "Good riddance," she muttered, with a wave of her hand, as she walked into the house.

Her future house.

Ever since her first visit to this dream house, which her friend had put together for years of enjoyment with her husband, Zorrie had envisioned herself as the lady of the house, with Kade Strong as her man. She felt no shame about that.

Zorrie and Reema had been friends since childhood, but Zorrie had always felt like she lived in Reema's shadow. Reema had been prettier, wealthier, and more popular. She had had more boyfriends, more dates, and more fun. Although Reema had always made sure to include her best friend, Zorrie had just lived with the jealousy for all those years.

In fact, Reema and Zorrie had been together at a high school party when they both met the handsome Kade. From the beginning, he had only had eyes for Reema. He had barely spared Zorrie a second glance, but she had secretly longed for him. Craved him. Wanted him.

Most of the time she was their third wheel, getting a firsthand view of all the wonderful things Kade did for her friend. She saw it all and wanted it all for herself. Even after she moved to North Carolina after college, she had thought of Kade and missed him something awful. She had wished things with him could've been different.

Zorrie slowly climbed the stairs, her hand trailing up the banister. She went into Kadina's bedroom and stood by her bed, looking down at the girl as she slept peacefully. "You should've been my little girl," she said softly as she bent over and smoothed the hair on Kadina's forehead. "Stepmother will be just fine."

She smiled in satisfaction before she left the room and made her way to Kade's bedroom. She inhaled deeply, with a soft moan, taking in the scent of him that still lingered in the room. She couldn't wait to share this space with Kade.

She pulled her nightgown over her head and slipped between the sheets of his bed, holding one of his pillows close to her nude body. She dug her face into the pillow and inhaled deeply. "Oh, Kade, why couldn't you see how much I loved you?" she whispered. "How much I still love you."

Zorrie had it all planned. She would keep being his friend and confidante and in time would become his lover and wife.

As she hugged the pillow and pressed it between her thighs, she looked at Kade and Reema's wedding photo. Her eyes shifted to the face of her childhood friend. "Don't worry, Reema. I'll take *real* good care of him for you."

Garcelle spent her day off giving the house a deep cleaning. Whenever she thought of that moment she'd shared with Kade on his porch, she scrubbed harder. She had wanted to kiss him so badly. So badly that she could still almost taste him.

She sat back on her heels in the bathroom and stared off at a nothing spot on the wall. Everything had become so complicated so quickly. Discovering that Kade might be feeling her the same way that she was feeling him just kicked it all up a notch. She had been catching all kinds of hell resisting him, but to have to resist a desire they *both* felt?

Kade Strong was not ready. Point blank.

There was a knock at the front door. Garcelle pushed away thoughts of steamy first kisses and naughty horseback rides as she walked to the living room. Her steps faltered when she looked through the glass screen door and saw Joaquin standing on the porch.

She had to admit that he was looking good even in a dusty T-shirt with the sleeves torn off and well-worn jeans. "What are you doing here, Joaquin?" she asked through the thin glass.

"I was dropping some of my crew home out here, and I saw your car," he said as his eyes cruised up and down her body in the terry-cloth strapless dress she wore.

Garcelle made an irritated face. "And?"

He flung his head back and laughed before he fixed his eyes on her. "Garcelle, why you always bustin' my balls?"

"Because you wanted to play with your balls in other *chicas*' playgrounds."

He pressed his hand to the door. "For real, Garcelle. Can't we start over? Can't we even be friends? Yo, we been through a lot, and I miss your ass, baby."

Garcelle saw the sincerity in his eyes. She motioned with her hands for him to back up; then she opened the door and stepped out onto the porch. "Sometimes I miss you, too, but I don't trust you no more."

"All I'm saying is give me another chance, Garcelle. Let me spend some time with you. I f'ed up, but I never cheated on you, and you know that."

"Joaquin . . ."

He reached out and took her hands in his. "Nothing serious then. Just a date. Let me take you to dinner or something."

Garcelle released a heavy breath. Joaquin was the only man she knew. He did hurt her when he ended their relationship, but only people you cared about had the power to hurt you. Maybe a few nights out on the town wouldn't be so bad. Joaquin might be just what she needed to get over Kade.

And get over him was exactly what she needed to do, because there was no way she could win a battle against the spirit of his dead wife.

The phone rang, and she slipped her hands out of his to walk into the house and answer it. "Hello."

"Garcelle, hey. This is Bianca. You busy?"

"What's up?" Garcelle turned her back to Joaquin.

"My dad's throwing a big cookout tomorrow, and I wanted to invite you and your family."

"You want me to bring something?" Garcelle offered.

"Nothing but those big old legs if you feel like dancing," Bianca joked.

Garcelle laughed. "I *always* feel like dancing, so I'll be there."

"I'm glad you're coming because we haven't seen each other in a minute."

Garcelle nodded as she turned back to eye Joaquin through the glass door. "Listen . . . Can I bring a date?"

Kade glanced at the time on his cell phone as he climbed the steps of his home. He and his crew had worked double time to finish up their work so that they would be able to attend the big cookout over at King Ranch. He was dusty and tired. His ribs had a dull ache, and he was starving.

He kicked off his boots at the front door and stripped as he made his way up the stairs and into his bedroom. Zorrie and Kadina were already at the cookout, so he had the house to himself. He walked through his open bedroom door.

"Kade!"

He looked up to find Zorrie walking out of his bathroom. He quickly covered his privates with his hands—as best he could—as she whirled around. "Zorrie, what the hell are you doing here?" he roared as he snatched the comforter from the bed and wrapped it around his waist.

"I thought it would be nice if I ran you a hot bath and got an outfit ready for you to wear to the cookout," she explained.

"Where's Kadina?" he asked, feeling annoyed.

"I left her at the cookout, with Garcelle," she said.

"Garcelle's there?" he asked. His stomach tightened at the thought of her.

"Are you still naked?" Zorrie asked.

"No."

She turned, holding a pair of his jeans and a shirt against her chest. He frowned when he noticed a pair of his boxers in her arms as well. She must have seen his aggravation, because she immediately set the items on his bed.

"The guy with her sure is good-looking."

Kade froze on his way to the bathroom. His head whipped around, and he pierced Zorrie with his eyes. "Garcelle brought a dude?" he asked, showing his surprise.

Zorrie nodded before she walked to the door. "She's an okay-looking girl. You sound surprised that she would have a boyfriend, Kade."

He thought of another man with Garcelle, and he

108 *Niobia Bryant*

couldn't deny that the rumbling in his stomach was nothing but the green-eyed monster . . . jealousy.

"You go ahead and get dressed. I'll just ride back over with you. No need for two cars," said Zorrie. She left the room, closing the door behind her.

But Kade barely paid her any mind as he dropped the comforter to the floor and walked into the bathroom. "Man, what the hell?"

The tub was indeed filled with water. He knew Zorrie was just trying to be helpful, but it was irritating to him that she had been in his room and in his clothes.

Not as irritating as seeing Garcelle with another man.

This thought seemed to pop out of nowhere. He had no right to feel so possessive about Garcelle. None at all.

He sat down on the edge of the tub and then reached down to lift the drain.

Podría enamorarme de ti muy, muy facilmente.

Kade's heart swelled in his chest at the memory of her words. He wished he knew the meaning. Regardless, the words had touched him. Just like the look in her eyes as they stood on that porch.

He'd felt that same intensity that day they first met, on Kahron's porch . . . and again when she took center stage, dancing at Kahron and Bianca's wedding reception. That day she had made him feel like she danced just for him.

The long muscle hanging down between his thighs stirred. The thought of Garcelle caused his blood to rush. When he rose to his feet, his penis hung heavily away from his muscled frame. The thought of Garcelle wanting him . . . desiring him . . . made him hard.

Kade massaged the full ten-inch length of it as he

stepped into the tub and turned the shower on full blast. He was glad for that first jolt of cool water before it warmed up. His hardness eased, but he knew it would take more than cold water to get Garcelle out of his system.

She had made him feel alive again.

Still . . . he was a man, not an animal. He was in control of his actions. He had no intention of pursuing Garcelle Santos. None at all.

9

The devil made me do it.

That was the only explanation Garcelle could give for why she'd chosen to wear the same crimson red sundress that she'd worn to Kahron and Bianca's wedding reception. Although she was normally dressed casually in shorts or jeans, she did have plenty of other more formal outfits she could have worn. Nothing but *el diablo* had made her reach in her closet for that dress.

Over the rim of her cup, Garcelle surveyed the large crowd of people enjoying the festivities on the front lawn and in the backyard of Hank King's home. She turned as she felt Joaquin's hand at the small of her back. It was an odd moment to discover that his touch of her bare skin did nothing to her. No shivers. No heat. No chemistry.

"Having fun . . . ?" asked Joaquin.

The rest of his words faded into nothing when she caught sight of Kade's SUV pulling into the yard. Her hand clutched her cup tighter as she suddenly felt thirsty and hot. Her breath caught in her throat as he parked and climbed out of the vehicle, in a

black polo and jeans. The color of his shirt empha-
sized his silver hair and the deep bronze of his skin.

She fanned herself with her hand as she took a
sip of her punch. Her eyes widened as Kade strode
around the SUV and opened the passenger door.
Those eyes hardened at the sight of him helping
Zorrie exit the vehicle. Those eyes pierced the
couple as they strode together toward the rest of
the partygoers.

When Kade looked in her direction from across
the yard, Garcelle held his stare for a long time,
before Zorrie said something to draw his attention.
Garcelle turned her back to them and reached up
to wipe an imaginary crumb from Joaquin's sculptured cheek.

Joaquin smiled as he slid his hand across her
back and pulled her a bit closer. He bent down to
whisper in her ear. "We look good together, Mami.
We'd make beautiful babies."

Nothing. Here she was with a gorgeous man who
she knew was great in bed, and she felt absolutely
nothing.

Garcelle leaned back to look into his eyes. "Nice
and slow. No rush, remember?"

Joaquin smiled and kissed her forehead. "Remember? You won't let me forget, beautiful."

"Bingo," she said, reaching down to entwine his
fingers with her own. She pulled him behind her.
"Let's go and get something to eat."

As they got in line to fix a plate from the buffet-
style spread, Garcelle didn't miss the odd expression her father gave her at seeing her and Joaquin
together. She ignored his eyes. If she wanted to
spend a little time with her ex-boyfriend, it wasn't
anyone's business but her own.

She glanced over her shoulder, and her eyes fell right on Kahron and Bianca laughing together. She looked away from them as jealousy gripped her like a vice.

Bianca left the kitchen to carry a platter of deviled eggs to the buffet table. She smiled at folks as she made her way over to the grill, where her father, Kahron, and a few older gentlemen were doing more talking and laughing than anything.

Kahron wrapped his arm around Bianca's shoulders when she reached his side. "Hey, B," he said.

Bianca kissed his cheek before she looked over his broad shoulder at the men loudly talking trash as they played whist inside the open garage. A Southern cookout wouldn't be a Southern cookout without a deck of fifty-two. "You're not playing?" she asked, knowing how much Kahron loved to play whist.

"Yeah, me and one of them Jamison twins are paired up," he said, sticking his hand inside the rear pocket of her snug jeans. "We got down behind the other Jamison twin and Kaleb."

She turned to her father. "Daddy, where's Mimi?" Bianca asked, looking around for what she was sure would be the loudest outfit ever created.

Hank grunted as he opened the lid of the industrial-sized grill. "I think she's still getting dressed. Go check on her for me," he requested as the smoke from the grill rose thickly around him.

"No problem," said Bianca. She gave Kahron a playful pinch on his buttocks before she went around the side of the house to the front. She smiled and waved at Anika and Chloe, the wives of the Jamison twins, who were walking together toward the rear of the house.

As she walked into the house, Bianca gave a friendly smile to a petite woman sitting alone on the porch.

"Bianca."

Bianca stepped back through the front door and onto the porch. "Yes?" she said politely as she looked down at the woman.

"It's me, sweetie."

Bianca's eyes widened as Mimi stood up before her. Bianca gasped as she circled Mimi and took it all in—or rather took in the lack of it all. Gone was the French roll, replaced by a more subdued ponytail. Mimi's face—her naturally pretty face—was free of all the layers of make-up. She wore a white tank and a pair of capris.

"Mi-mi," Bianca said in astonishment. My God, you're a foot shorter without that big old hairdo."

Mimi crossed her arms over her chest. "Stick to being a vet, because comedy isn't your forte," she said in a husky voice. "Listen, I need to talk to you—"

Bianca stepped back as her mouth dropped open, and she pointed accusingly at Mimi. "What happened to your voice?"

Mimi grabbed Bianca's hand. "Can you be any louder, or should I get you a mic and a spotlight?" she snapped sarcastically.

Bianca looked around and saw that a few sets of eyes were indeed on them.

Mimi continued. "Listen. I really like your father, and I want this to work, and . . . I know I can be over the top with the whole Mimi thing. And . . . and . . . to be honest, since your daddy came into my life, I don't even want to put on any more—"

Bianca was confused, and she knew it showed on her face. "Mimi, are you drunk?"

"No," Mimi snapped forcibly. "You know what, Bianca? Never mind. To hell with it."

Mimi brushed past her and walked down the stairs and over to Hank. Bianca was left to wonder what *she* had done to anger Mimi.

"Aren't those two a mess?" Lisha Strong asked her sons Kaeden and Kaleb when she walked up to them.

Both of the men nodded without asking for further explanation. There wasn't a need for any. For the last thirty minutes, they'd watched Kade and Garcelle play the game of staring at each other openly and watching the other without letting the other know what they were doing.

"It's so obvious they want each other that they're making me warm under the collar just watching them," Kaleb drawled before he tilted his head back to empty the can of beer he held.

"Don't you just love it," Lisha said, with delight, as she watched Kade and Garcelle share another heated stare.

No matter how much he forced himself to look away from her, his eyes eventually sought and found Garcelle. Kade couldn't take his eyes off of her. Nothing else held his attention. As the sun set and the skies darkened, he watched her. As the crowd began to thin in numbers, he watched her. In fact, he was glad when his sister came and pulled Zorrie from his side to socialize with the rest of the women in the front yard.

And this desire to look at her was nothing new. Ever since that dance at the wedding reception—if not before—he'd found himself sneaking looks at her. Here she was in *that* dress. Just the sight of it on her curves made him sweat. When she was in old jeans and a T-shirt, there was no denying her beauty, but in *that* dress, she took his breath away.

Garcelle smiled up at her date and placed her hand on his chest as he kissed her temple. Kade clenched his jaw. He wished that he could be that man by her side, feeling her touch, receiving her smiles.

Kade saw that when her eyes hit him over her date's shoulder, her smile disappeared. They were zoned in to each other.

He knew he should look away . . . but he couldn't. Whenever his eyes locked with hers, it felt like no one else existed. Just he and Garcelle. Even across the twenty yards separating them, he felt the same electricity and fire crackle between them.

He hadn't felt that way for a woman since Reema.

Her date, Mr. Rico Suave, stepped in their direct line of vision, and Kade released a shaky breath as if he had been held captive by a spell. "Damn," he swore quietly.

"You two want to get in each other's pants so bad," Kaleb said as he walked up to where his brother stood alone. "Funny thing is . . . Everyone here seems to know it *except* you two."

"You don't know what you're talking about." Kade crushed his empty beer can in his hand.

Kaleb laughed. "Okay. Then maybe Mama, Kaeden, Kahron, and Bianca know what *they're* talking about, because I've had this same conversation with all of them. I drew the short straw to tell your ass to stop staring so hard or make a move, for God's sake."

Kade directed his eyes toward everything—anything—*but* Garcelle and Rico Suave. "Why the hell are you so talkative tonight?"

"Can't say I blame you for wanting her," Kaleb said, ignoring Kade's sarcasm. "I would be more than happy to tap that—"

Kade spun and grabbed Kaleb by the front of his shirt. His eyes were filled with anger . . . until he saw that his younger brother was laughing at him. Kaleb had goaded him right into a trap.

"You're wearing your heart on your sleeve, big brother," Kaleb said in a slow Southern drawl as he calmly reached over his brother's arm to take a deep sip of his beer.

Kade released him just as roughly as he had jacked him up. "Mind your business," he growled before he walked away from his brother.

From her spot in the front yard, Garcelle watched the scene unfold between Kade and his brother. Kade walked farther in the back and out of her view. When she shifted her eyes to Kaleb, he held up his can of beer in a salute to her before he strolled away, with a smile.

She turned her head again, and she saw Zorrie, Lisha, and Kade's sister, Kaitlyn, talking as they looked in her direction. Lisha's and Kaitlyn's eyes were warm and amused, but if looks could kill, Zorrie would have dropped her in the blink of an eye.

"Something wrong?" Joaquin asked, looking down at her.

"No," she told him, even though her thoughts were full of Kade.

She was with another man and hadn't been within five feet of Kade, and he *still* sent her pulse racing with one look. "I'll be right back," she told Joaquin, needing a moment to herself.

Garcelle made her way through the crowd and climbed the stairs to the house. She almost walked into Bianca, who was leaving the house.

"Garcelle . . . Garcelle . . . Garcelle," Bianca said teasingly.

"What?"

Bianca grabbed her hand. "Well, I need to talk to you, Mamasita," she said over her shoulder as she pulled Garcelle behind her and into the kitchen.

"Slow down, Bianca," Garcelle said as she almost tripped over her own feet.

"Okay, so tell me. What kind of spell have you put on my brother-in-law?"

Garcelle walked around the kitchen, pretending she was more interested in the decor than she actually was. "I am so glad your father redecorated in here. It looks much better than that mess your ex-stepmother had in here. Did you help him pick the new colors?"

"Oh no, Garcelle, you're stalling."

Garcelle sat at the island and stared at her friend. "Is your daddy dating that *loca* lady Mimi?" she countered, deliberately changing the subject again.

"Touché," Bianca said, with a laugh. "I'm not happy about it all. I love my friend, but I don't think she's right for my father. I just haven't worked up the nerve to tell them how I feel. Okay, so I've said my peace. Your turn."

Garcelle shrugged. "Okay, Ms. Nosy. I think Kade

Strong is the sexiest man I have ever laid these eyes on. He makes my heart go really fast, you know."

"I knew it!" Bianca slammed her hand down against the island top.

"*But* . . . he still loves his wife, and there is no chance for us," Garcelle said sadly.

Bianca reached for her hand. "Maybe you can be the woman to pull him out of his mourning. Do you love him?"

Garcelle shook her head. "No, I would be lying if I said I was *in* love, but I do care about him. He's such a good father to Kadina, and he's really good and fair to his workers. I like him a lot."

"And you want him bad, don't you?"

"I do have naughty dreams of having sex with him in odd places . . . like riding him on top of a horse." Garcelle's cheeks warmed at her admission.

Bianca bit on the tip of her index finger as she looked off into the distance, with a reflective expression. "Kahron and I have done some things, but . . . on horseback, huh?"

"*Sí*, horseback."

Both women did a high five before they fanned themselves.

Zorrie saw Garcelle's date, sans Garcelle, in the backyard, with the rest of the men. Her heart raced as her eyes sought out Kade. She felt relief when she saw him standing on the sidelines, watching the men play cards. For a moment, she thought he had snuck off with Garcelle.

Everyone at the cookout was buzzing about the obvious attraction between Kade and Garcelle. Zorrie hadn't missed their long stares and clandestine peeks at one another. She knew for sure that Kade was sniffing around Garcelle's hot-blooded skirts.

Zorrie wasn't too concerned. Garcelle was a Latin servant . . . good enough to screw, but not to marry. No, in the end, Kade would want a proper woman as his wife. Namely, her. And she planned to see that it happened sooner rather than later.

Kade was quiet for the rest of the night. He had a lot on his mind. Or at least someone was on his mind a lot.

"Damn, Kade. Pay attention, man," Kaleb complained as he counted their tricks. "They got a two."

Kade winced at the score. In whist, there were thirteen tricks up for grabs. With the two teams playing against each other, any trick over six was a win. And then each trick over six was counted as the score. Their opponents ran a two, meaning they had eight tricks to their five.

"My bad, man," said Kade.

"Shit. Not your bad. Our good, baby. Don't sweat that," one of the Jamison twins joked as he reached across the table to give Kahron a dap.

"We just need a one to send them from here. Let's get to work," Kahron added as he pushed his shades up on his head.

Kaleb grumbled as he dealt a new hand. "Pay attention, and get your mind off of you know who," he said, with a hard stare at his older brother.

As Kade arranged his hand, he looked up and saw Carlos Santos walk up and stand behind Kaleb. "Carlos, what does *podría enamorarme de ti muy, muy facilmente* mean?"

"Man, what the hell are you talking about now?"

Kaleb said, with attitude, as he dropped his hand to the table.

Kade ignored him. His body was tense as he looked at the older man.

"It means 'I could fall in love with you so very, very easily.'"

Kade felt a chill race over his body.

10

Two Weeks Later

Dozens of spotlights filtered through red film shown on the lone figure sitting in the middle of the dance floor. Kade's arms were tied behind his back as he sat completely . . . and devastatingly . . . nude. His tall and muscular frame seemed to dominate the wooden chair as he calmly waited. Fine silver hair highlighted the strong contours of his chest, dwindling to a fine line through his rigid abdomen and then spreading out to cover and surround the thick root of his dark penis, hanging between his open thighs.

A soft and sultry Spanish song began to play, and the fine hairs on his body stood on end. The muscle between his thighs stirred to life. His heart pounded.

Garcelle came spiraling toward him in that crimson red dress, and their eyes locked when she stopped dramatically before him, with a flirty smile. She bent over to hotly trace his lips with her skillful tongue. She laughed huskily as he jostled about in the chair in an effort to free his tied hands.

His solid penis rose to attention as she slid her hands from his broad shoulders and down the length of his chest before she moved to stand behind him. She pressed her *breasts to the back of his neck as her hand descended and surrounded his steel inches. She stroked upward in a rhythmic motion.*

"Please, Garcelle," he begged as he tilted his head back against her bosom.

She jiggled her breasts against him before she stepped back. She loved how he twisted and turned in the chair to get her in his line of vision. She moved back around him as the tempo of the music quickened. She shook her hair free, letting it spill down over her shoulders, before she slid down to the floor in a frontward split.

Kade's eyes burned a hole through her soul as she lifted her voluminous dress skirt to show him how she lightly worked her hips up and down as if riding the floor like a lover. His penis bobbed like a diving board as he clenched the muscles of his abdomen.

Garcelle rose to her feet, releasing the dress skirt, and it floated down around her hips and thighs as she removed the straps of her dress. They fell from her softly rounded shoulders with ease, exposing her small, but firm and plump, breasts to his eager eyes.

His mouth gaped open as his heart pounded wildly in his chest. She swiveled her hips as she used her thumbs to work the dress down her hips. It fell with a whoosh down her thick, shapely legs to the floor.

Kade's penis ached at the sight of her nakedness. "Come ride me," he ordered thickly as sweat covered his body.

Garcelle brought her hands up to play lightly in the soft and neat curls covering her core. She walked to him, with the strength and grace of a panther. "Are you ready for me now?" she asked in a thick Spanish accent.

He tilted his head back to look up at her with heat- and desire-filled eyes. "More than ready."

She straddled his hips, shifting forward so that the hard base of his penis pressed against the thick lips of her moist *opening. She used her hands to guide one pert breast to his open, eager, and ready mouth.*

As Kade's tongue circled her chocolate nipple, Garcelle rose up on her toes and held his heat with her shaking hand as she eased down upon it, with a harsh intake of breath.

He clenched his jaw and furrowed his brow as his hips bucked upward, off the chair, at the feel of her tightly surrounding him. Throbbing against him. Soaking him with her juices. "Garcelle," he roared.

She arched her back, her head nearly reaching the floor, as she worked her hips and rode him. At times she worked his shaft slow and sensual. At other times she was fast and furious.

The muscles in his arms, shoulders, and back tightened as he pulled against the bonds holding him. With one final savage grunt, he tore the material that secured him, and he was free to touch her.

He didn't use those hands to grab at her buttocks or breasts but to pull her upper body to him before he lightly grasped the sides of her face. "Podría enamorarme de ti muy, muy facilmente," he whispered to her tenderly.

Tears filled Garcelle's eyes as she lowered her head to kiss him deeply. . . .

Garcelle eyes fluttered open as she shook off her hot daydream. When she touched her cheeks, she wasn't surprised to find that like in her heated and emotional dream, she was crying. Everything had seemed so real.

The sex. The emotions. His words. She sighed.

In the last two weeks, her relationship with Kade had gone from awkward to distant to near nonexistent. They only saw each other in passing. He had even started leaving her paycheck on the counter in the kitchen. She wouldn't be surprised if he let her go from the job next.

That would probably make Zorrie Kintrell climax all over herself. Somehow the woman's vacation had been extended to a whole month. Didn't she have a job to get back to?

Okay. In truth, what really had her going was the obvious closeness she saw developing between the woman and Kade. Correction. Between Zorrie, Kade, *and* Kadina.

Thankfully, Zorrie was visiting the house less and less during the day. Just when Garcelle thought the woman had found her life, she discovered Zorrie saved her "visits" for the evening . . . when Kade was home. Like clockwork, little Kadina would innocently fill Garcelle in on all the fun the threesome had had the night before . . . at dinner, the movies, the local fairs and festivals, the water parks, etc., etc.

To Garcelle, Zorrie was the worst of the worst man hunters, because she was going after the husband of her dead best friend *and* she was using a sweet, innocent child to do it. "*Puta*," Garcelle muttered under her breath as she walked over to the window to check on Kadina, who was riding her bike in the front yard.

Kade was blind if he didn't see MANIPULATOR and HORNY MAN HUNTER written all over Zorrie's pretty and vacant face. It frustrated her so much that she felt like climbing to the top of the house and scream down at him, "Get your head out of your ass, Kade Strong."

Then again, maybe Zorrie Kintrell was what Kade wanted. He was pulling further and further away from their newfound friendship and closer to Zorrie. The woman's personality was as flat as paint.

If Garcelle had to spend more than an hour in her presence, she felt herself getting sleepy. Seriously.

"Whatever," Garcelle said, with a false nonchalance, as she reached into the double-sided refrigerator for the bowl of chicken salad she'd made earlier to serve for lunch. She was busying herself with making Kadina a sandwich, with sliced fresh fruit for dessert, when she heard the front door open and close.

"I was just about to call you in for lunch, Kadina," she said over her shoulder as she reached in the fridge for one of the little girl's juice boxes.

"I'm not Kadina, but I could go for lunch if you're offering."

At the sound of Kade's voice and the knowledge of his presence, Garcelle closed her eyes and took a deep, steadying breath as she clutched that juice box until the middle caved in. "Right away, Mr. Strong," she said, with an edge in her voice.

"Mr. Strong?"

Garcelle ignored his question and began to fix him a sandwich. "Do you want chicken salad or tuna fish?" she asked. "Or should I call Zorrie and ask her to tell you what you want?"

Kade looked over his shoulder at her as he washed his hands at the sink. He frowned. "Zorrie?"

Garcelle waved her hand dismissively. "Nothing."

Kade dried his hands with a towel as he swaggered over to her. "No, say whatever you have to say. Be a woman about yours."

Garcelle eyed him sharply as he stood beside her, but she chose to say nothing. *Kade Strong and Zorrie Kintrell are none of my concern. I just work here.*

"Speak up, Garcelle. I've never known you to be so

quiet," he said sarcastically as he moved over to the island and jerked one of the stools back to sit on.

"And I've never known you to be so . . . so . . . blind," she flipped back at him before she could catch herself.

Kade jumped to his feet and slammed his hand against the top of the island as he pierced her with his eyes. "Say what you gotta say, Garcelle."

She swallowed back everything she wanted to tell him. "I like my job, so eat your sandwich while I go and get Kadina," she told him, flinging the dish towel onto the counter as she walked past him to leave the kitchen.

He reached out and caught her wrist.

Garcelle yanked her wrist free of his grasp, with eyes blazing, as she faced him. "Two weeks ago on your porch, you started to kiss me, and I was woman enough to tell you that you were not ready, Kade Strong. Now you're dating your wife's best friend—"

Kade's eyes flared as he leaned down to Garcelle. "I'm not dating anybody," he spit out.

"Hah!" Garcelle said, with a sarcastic laugh. "If a man and a woman go out to eat, to the movies, and all that good stuff . . . they *are* dating, baby."

Kade flung his hands in the air.

"That woman is a barracuda in disguise. A wolf in sheep's clothing . . . ," cried Garcelle.

Kade turned his back to her as he reclaimed his seat. "You don't even know her to have an opinion about her."

"Hell, do you really know her?"

"Better than you know your boyfriend, Rico Suave, I bet," he countered around a mouthful of his sandwich.

"Rico Suave?" Garcelle came around the island to face him. "Is that a racist comment?"

Kade dropped his sandwich on his plate. "Oh God, not *that* shit again."

"What? You don't like Latinos?"

"I . . . am . . . not . . . a racist!" Kade yelled at the top of his lungs. "And you know that, Garcelle."

Yeah, she did, but so what.

"You ain't a good judge of character, either, baby," she said under her breath as she moved away from him.

"Zorrie is a good friend of mine and nothing more."

"Keep dating your wife's best friend. I don't care," she said dismissively as she started putting things back in the refrigerator.

Kade came up behind her, and Garcelle felt the heat of his body cloak her. When his hands came around to cover her hands, she thought she would pass out from wanting him so bad.

"You care," he said huskily. "Just like I hate seeing you with ole boy."

Garcelle allowed herself to lean back against the hardness of his body.

"But I am not dating Zorrie or anyone else, because you're right . . . I'm not ready."

Those words pained her so very deeply.

He pressed the side of his face to hers as he whispered, "If I did date, it would be you, Garcelle. It would be you. *Only* you."

Her heart hammered, and she felt weak as her core moistened.

The front door slammed, and Kadina's footsteps echoed in the hall. Kade and Garcelle moved apart. The sudden distance did nothing to stop her racing pulse or the heady thump-thump of the pulsing bud between her legs.

Kadina burst into the kitchen, dripping wet, just as thunder roared and clapped around the house. "It started raining, just like you said, Daddy."

Garcelle and Kade both laughed at the sight she made.

"You look like a drowned squirrel, cupcake," Kade said, reaching out to lightly pinch her nose. "I told you it called for rain this afternoon."

"It started all of a sudden," Kadina said as she smiled up at him like he was her hero.

"Go and get out of those wet clothes before you catch a cold," Garcelle told her.

"I'll be right back," Kadina told them before she tore off at a full run.

As soon as she left them alone, Garcelle felt Kade's eyes rest on her. "So you're off for the rest of the day?" she asked, trying to sound normal so that maybe she could convince herself that this whole situation *was* normal.

"Yeah. Looks like I got home just in time to beat the rain."

Garcelle chanced a look at him, and her heart responded in a flash. "Since you're home, I'm going to cut out and go home early if that's okay."

Kade nodded as he took a halfhearted bite of his sandwich. "Are you leaving early because of me?" he asked in a low voice.

Garcelle grabbed her purse and keys from the counter. "Tell Kadina I'll see her tomorrow. Tell her we'll go to one of the ranches and ride horses," she said quietly before she strode out of the kitchen, completely ignoring his question.

Garcelle walked out the front door. The rain was

coming down so heavily that it looked like the windows had been smeared with Vaseline. She paused on the porch, trying to decide if she should wait it out until the rain lightened or just make a run for her car.

The front door opened behind her, and she looked over her shoulder at Kade. They shared another one of those long, hot stares before she turned away. He stepped onto the porch, beside her.

The slight chill from the rain left her, from being so close to him. He reached for her hand, but Garcelle dodged his touch. She looked up at him, and their eyes locked. She felt herself getting lost in the depths of him. She did a full turn to break the hold. "Good-bye, Kade," she said in frustration before she dashed down the steps, into the pouring rain.

Just as she reached her car, she felt a hand on her shoulder, turning her around. The rain pelted their bodies, drenching them both. He brought his hands up to her face to tilt it forward as he lowered his head to hers. They pressed their mouths together. Garcelle closed her eyes as she raised her hands and wrapped them around each of his wrists.

Steam could have risen from the heat of their bodies as they shared a slow and sensual kiss. Their tongues tentatively touched for the first time before circling and suckling as they stepped closer to each other. They both trembled. Their hands shook. She felt his hardness. He knew he had made her wet.

Garcelle broke the kiss as she panted for air. "Don't, Kade," she warned.

"Don't what?" he repeated.

"*You've* said you're not ready. *I've* said you're not

ready. So no more long stares or kisses or touches or standing close or any of that."

"Garcelle—"

"This isn't all about you and you trying to deal with your wife's death, Kade. I have feelings. All the looks, that kiss, all of that affects me, and then I have to deal with you pulling away because you're not ready. I can tell you're torn, but I have to look out for me, you know. So unless you want me to quit working for you, just stop. Stop. Please."

Kade nodded as he reached for the keys and unlocked her car door. "You're right, and I'm sorry," was all that he said.

Garcelle climbed into the car. She watched as he walked up the stairs and into the house, without looking back at her.

Kade had forgotten how much he enjoyed sitting beside the lit stone fireplace in his den. Sometimes he'd read; other times he'd watch television. Today he sat quietly, reflecting as he watched the rain shower outside his window. He let his head fall back against the leather club chair where he sat as he twisted the gold wedding band on his finger.

He had a lot on his mind. Memories. Regrets. Desires. His past. His present. His future.

"Daddy, whatcha doing?"

He looked up as Kadina walked into the den in her Dora the Explorer pajamas, wiping the sleep from her eyes. His heart swelled with love for his child. "Just chilling. You had a good nap?"

She nodded. "I always get sleepy when it's raining," she told him as she climbed up to sit on the wide arm of the chair. She hooked her feet beneath his leg.

"You got that from your mama." Kade turned his head to look at his daughter. "A day like today? She could sleep all day."

"We don't talk about her a lot." Kadina reached for his hand to play with. "Does it make you sad, Daddy?"

"Not as much," he answered truthfully. "Does it make you sad to talk about her?"

Kadina shook her head. "Talking about her makes me remember stuff about her, and that don't make me sad at all, Daddy."

"Then I think we should talk about her more often." Kade tickled her sides, and the sound of her laughter filled him with joy.

"You know what, Daddy?" Kadina asked as she reached up to twist her fingers around his naturally curly silver hair.

"What?"

"I like when Garcelle and Aunt Zorrie are here, or when my uncles and auntie come over, but I like when it's just me and you."

Kade raised himself a bit in the seat to kiss her forehead. "Me, too, cupcake," he told her. "In fact, Aunt Zorrie was supposed to come by and bring some movies for us to watch, but why don't we call her and tell her we're gonna chill out tonight. Just me and you."

Kadina's eyes lit up. "Can we order pizza?"

"We can do whatever you want." Kade reached in the pocket of his sweatpants for his cell phone.

"Are you calling Aunt Zorrie now?"

Kade nodded. "Unless you've changed your mind."

She shook her head. "At first I thought Aunt

Zorrie was here to see me, but I think she just wants to see you."

From the mouths of babes.

First Garcelle and now his daughter. Couldn't a man and a woman just be friends?

11

Garcelle used the rubber band on her wrist to pull her hair up into a ponytail before she reached into the dryer for the warm load of clothes. She dumped them into the basket and made her way through the kitchen and up the stairs to Kadina's bedroom. "Excited about spending the weekend with your grandparents?" she asked as she sat the basket on the end of Kadina's twin-size bed.

Kadina was sitting on the lavender window seat, looking out at the clouds. "I guess," she said, with a sad tone in her voice.

Garcelle folded the last piece of Kadina's clothes and pressed it down into her rolling overnight case. She sat on the window seat, beside Kadina. "Something wrong?"

"I hate leaving Daddy all by himself."

Garcelle reached out to stroke Kadina's head before she lightly tugged on her ponytail. "Trust me. Your papi will be just fine for the weekend while you're in Walterboro with your *abuelos*."

"I tried to get him to go to the horse race with Uncle Kahron. Uncle Kahron always says he has fun."

Garcelle nodded. "Yes, my father, uncles, and my little brother went as well."

"I wish Daddy woulda went."

"I'm sure your father will be just fine," Garcelle said.

"I guess."

Garcelle rose and moved back over to the bed to zip Kadina's overnight case and sit it by her bedroom door. "This is a nice picture," she said, picking up the five-by-seven picture frame holding a photo of two teenage girls and a teenage boy.

"Auntie Zorrie gave it to me." Kadina pulled her knees to her chest as she picked at an old scab. "It's my mama, Aunt Zorrie, and Daddy when they were younger."

Garcelle lightly touched Kade's smiling face with her index finger. It was odd to see him young and thin, with jet-black curls. He was younger, but the promise of his handsomeness in his adult years was already there. She sat the frame back down on the corner of the dresser. "They've been friends for a long time," she said before she went over and straightened the few wrinkles in the comforter on Kadina's bed.

"Aunt Zorrie said she was there when Daddy met my mom," Kadina said. "She used to always tell me a lot of stuff I didn't know about my mom. They were best friends."

Garcelle looked up at her. "Used to?"

"Now she changes the subject when I ask her things about my mom. She always wants to talk about Daddy."

I bet she does, Garcelle thought as she tooted up her mouth. "Let's head to the ranch."

Kadina jumped to her feet and slid her book in the side pocket of her overnight case. "Garcelle?"

Garcelle led Kadina out of the room and down the stairs. "Yeah?"

"Are you and my daddy mad?"

Garcelle paused as she held the front door open. "Uh . . . no, of course not. Why?"

They continued down the stairs and out the front door. "You guys don't talk much," Kadina said as she got into the backseat of Garcelle's car.

"Your dad and I are cool as ever, sweetheart," Garcelle lied. She and Kade had deliberately not shared each other's immediate space since that day in the rain. "Top down?"

Kadina buckled her seat belt. "*Sí. Gracias.*"

Garcelle smiled at her as she worked on lowering and securing the manual convertible top.

"I wouldn't want you and Daddy to be mad," Kadina continued.

Garcelle hopped into the car, and soon they were headed down the long and bumpy drive to the main road. "Me, either," she said, more focused on checking for oncoming traffic before she made a right turn onto Highway 17 and headed to Walterboro.

"You two should kiss and make up."

Garcelle eyed the little girl in the rearview mirror, with an alarmed expression. "Grown-ups don't kiss and make up."

"Grown-ups who like each other do."

Garcelle said nothing, wanting the whole conversation to end.

"Everybody knows you and Daddy like each other like girlfriend and boyfriend."

Garcelle nearly slammed on the brakes. "I work for your father. That's all."

She felt the tension finally ease from her body as Kadina fell quiet on the subject. She turned on the radio and sped toward their destination.

"Garcelle, if you was my new mommy, would I speak Spanish like my friend Maria?"

Oh my God. This little girl is a pit bull about this.

Garcelle pulled the car to a stop in front of the spacious brick home of Kael and Lisha Strong. "Okay, we're here," she said cheerfully, with way too much enthusiasm.

The front door opened, and Lisha stepped out onto the porch, dressed in a long jean skirt and a lime green T-shirt. "There's my grandbaby!"

Garcelle grabbed Kadina's overnight case as the little girl went flying up the stairs to fling her arms around her grandmother's waist.

"Garcelle, you better put that hood up. The weatherman is calling for rain," Lisha called down to her.

"I wasn't staying—"

"Of course, you are. It's lunchtime. Come on in," Lisha said over her shoulder before she followed Kadina into the house.

The scent of well-seasoned food mingled in the air with the natural aromas of the ranch. The smell of the food won out, and Garcelle's stomach growled in frustration. *A stop at Taco Bell will take care of that,* she thought as she glanced up at the sky and saw the dark storm clouds overshadowing the blue skies. She decided that putting up the top while she was stationary was a good idea.

After moving to South Carolina, she had learned early that rain was a natural occurrence. It could be blue skies and sunshine one moment and grey skies and rain the next.

At the sound of horse hooves, she turned and saw

Kade and his father ride up together. She had to force her eyes off the impressive sight Kade made in the saddle.

"*Hola,*" she greeted them as she snapped the hood of her car in place as they both climbed down off their stallions with ease.

"How have you been, Garcelle?" Kael asked as he handed the reins of his horse to Kade.

"Real good. And you?" said Garcelle.

"Just fine . . . just fine," said Kael as he climbed the stairs of the porch. He turned on the top step and looked down at her, with assessing eyes. He turned his head a bit to give his son a long, meaningful, hard stare before he walked into the house, with a shake of his silver head.

Garcelle thought she heard him say, "Never thought I'd have a mule for a son. Damndest thing."

She tried her best to ignore Kade, but she felt him standing there, looking at her. "Tell your mom I couldn't stay for lunch, but thanks, anyway," she said in a rush to Kade before she jumped into her car and sped away like she was driving a race car.

"He's going after her," Lisha said from her spot at the left side of the living room window.

"That mule-headed son of ours? No way," Kael replied from his spot at the right side of the same window.

"Go after her, Daddy," said Kadina as she watched from her spot in the middle.

They all peered out as Kade turned to eye Garcelle's car as it sped away. He ran his hand through his hair and kicked the dirt with his boot before he turned amid the flying dust and climbed the stairs to the house.

"Go . . . go . . . go," Lisha urged them as they all scattered from the window before they were caught being nosey.

It was after seven when Kade left Walterboro and headed home. Halfway down Highway 17, the skies opened up, the winds increased in velocity, and he found himself in the middle of a storm. As the rain made anything more than a foot ahead of him disappear, he slowed down to a creeping ten miles per hour.

He was glad when he finally pulled into his puddle-filled yard and dashed into the house. Stripping off the wet clothing by the front door, he carried the bundle into the washroom, located off the kitchen. He took his cell phone and wallet from the pants before he dumped them into the washing machine. The wind rattled the house. Lightning and thunder fought for dominance.

In his room he turned on the lights and hurried into an old pair of sweatpants and a T-shirt. He used the remote to turn on the TV in the corner. He dried his hair with a towel as he listened to the latest weather update on the local Live 5 news.

"There is a thunderstorm warning and a tornado watch in the following areas. . . ."

"A tornado watch?" He dropped down on the bottom of the bed and watched the colorful maps.

"SCE&G are reporting electrical outages. Nearly five hundred customers are currently without power. . . ."

Kade frowned as he rose and grabbed a pair of socks from the dresser drawer.

"Again, if you are in a mobile home, it is best to find more secure shelter, and if you are in a stable home, try to stay close to the center of the home in case the tornado touches down in your area. Wind gusts are currently up to . . ."

Garcelle. His face became pensive as he thought of her alone in that mobile home when there was a chance of a tornado touching down in Holtsville. The thought nagged at him. He snatched up his cordless phone and dialed her home number.

"Hello."

"Garcelle?"

"Kade?"

"Are you okay? I know you're home alone in all of this—"

The line filled with static, and then the call was disconnected completely.

He tried to dial her back but got only a busy signal. He didn't think twice as he rushed into a pair of sneakers and snatched up his keys, cell phone, and wallet. He flew down the stairs and out the door and into the storm.

Garcelle gasped as the lights flickered off. Her family was away to attend the horserace, so she was home alone in the dark. She dropped the cordless phone, knowing it was useless without power. The wind whipped against the house, causing it to sway just a bit. She was alarmed. She was nervous. She wasn't crazy.

She already had candles situated throughout the house. She reached into her back pocket for the lighter. She decided to light only the candles in the living room, where she could keep an eye on them. With the swaying of the house, the candles could fall over and start a fire.

She chanced a glance out the window. "Aw shit," she whispered at the sights unfolding before her. Her mouth opened in awe and shock. The winds were causing the trees to bend until the tops touched the ground. Random items, like garbage cans, flower-pots, beer cans, and trash, soared through the air like Frisbees. A plastic lid to a garbage can was flung against the glass door, causing her to jump back nearly a foot before she scrambled to close and lock the big front door.

She was wishing frugality hadn't won out when she'd debated buying a cell phone when headlights flashed against the living-room wall. A car was in the yard! She jumped up from the sofa and peeked out the door. She flung it open wide at the sight of Kade's Expedition. He dashed out of the vehicle, and she opened the screen door, wincing as the rain immediately pelted her legs, which were ex-posed in the shorts she wore.

"Kade," she said as he stepped through the door. He threw an arm around her waist and picked her up, pressing her body against his. She felt his heart hammering against her chest as she wrapped her arms around his neck tightly.

In that moment, being in his arms felt right.

He pressed his face into her neck. "I was wor-ried. Damn, the ride over here was the longest ride of my life."

She nodded as she felt him plant kisses along the length of her neck.

Kade brought his lips up to her cheek and then

to her lips. "I need you, Garcelle. I've been trying fight it, but I do . . . I need you. I need you," he whispered against her mouth.

They stared deep into each other's eyes as the candles flickered and the storm raged around them. In unison, they brought their heads closer to share soft and gentle kisses. It seemed like they shared a hundred of them. Maybe a thousand. Maybe more.

"I have to have you in my life, Garcelle. I miss you when you're not around the house. I think about you all the time." Kade dropped his head to Garcelle's panting chest. "You make me happy, and I *deserve* to be happy."

"Yes," she sighed in pleasure as she brought her hands up to hold his handsome face. "I can make you happy, Kade. I want to make you happy. I want to be in your life and spend time with you. Make love with you. Have fun with you. But, baby, are your ready? Because I don't want to be hurt."

Kade dropped to his knees, bringing Garcelle with him. He pressed her down to the carpeted floor, then slipped his hand under her T-shirt to squeeze her soft breasts. "I'm ready, Garcelle. I'm ready," he whispered into her open mouth before he kissed her deeply as lightning flashed outside, briefly illuminating the house.

Garcelle's hands fumbled a bit as she tugged his damp shirt over his head. Her hips writhed as he grinded his hips against her, sending his hardness sliding up and down against the wetness of her core until she thought she would come. She placed her hands on kis shoulders and pushed him back onto the floor. She shifted so that she straddled him. She sat up straight and lifted her shirt over her head. Her breasts jiggled a bit as she freed them.

Kade's breath caught in his chest as she licked her fingers before teasing her own nipples, with a purr. "What the . . . ," he whispered.

Garcelle bent her legs, exposing her core to him as she sat astride him. She slid her own hands down the length of her body to play in her slick, wet folds. One finger disappeared in the warm depths. She pulled it from her core, and it glistened before she sucked her own juices from that lucky finger.

Kade felt a fine layer of sweat coat his body. Never had his clothes felt so restrictive. Never had he wanted to bury himself so deeply inside a woman's walls.

She writhed against the base of his hardness, and Kade winced a bit at the feel of her softness against his aching dick. His hands instinctively rose to grab her waist. Her skin was soft and warm. Perfect. She grinded against him until he felt the moistness of her intimacy dampen his pants. She looked down at him with clouded eyes. "Kiss me," she demanded as she reached behind for his hands and slid them down to her buttocks.

Kade felt caught in her web. His heart pounded, its beat distinct from the pulsating of his dick. He let his eyes drop to the fullness of her mouth. Yes, he would like to kiss her lips and her breasts and the rose petal–like lips and clit of her core.

"You are beautiful," he whispered into that intimate space between them as his chin rose. Never before had he felt so taken by a woman so quickly and so easily.

The thick muscle between his thighs pushed deeply against her softness. It throbbed and ached to nuzzle between her lips and pink flesh until her walls clutched him.

She laughed coquettishly before she bent down and brought her hands up to hold his face and pressed her lips to his.

Kade's control broke at the feel of her tongue probing his lips. He allowed her tongue to slip through his heated lips before she drew his own into her mouth with ease as she worked her hips like they were not under her control.

"Make love to me, Kade," she said into his open mouth as she looked into his eyes with clear intent.

"I damn sure will," he answered as he rolled her over and pressed her body down on the floor. He stripped her, with urgency in his movements, before he rose to his knees.

Garcelle's eyes caressed his features as he removed his clothing and stood between her open legs, naked and virile. He was beautiful. Strong. Sexy. Confident.

She was consumed by the desire to push him back down to the floor and slide down onto every delicious inch of his rod until his hairs tickled her buttocks. She wanted to ride him until she drained every bit of hardness from him.

Garcelle purred, feeling high with desire as she spread her legs wider, massaged the curves of her body, then played in the slick, wet folds between her quivering thighs. "I want you now, Kade," she insisted, looking up into his handsome face.

"I can tell," he teased, his eyes seeming to pierce hers as his hands moved up her squirming body to massage the full, luscious globes of her breasts with supreme skill, making her gasp sharply as chills racked her body. His fingers lightly teased and plucked her thick nipples between deep massages.

"Feel good?" he asked thickly.

"So good," she answered.

His long and hard penis hung heavily from his body, and she shivered as it lightly brushed against her thigh when he bent his upper body down over hers. Blindly, she reached for it, stroking his heat as he lightly circled her nipple with his tongue.

Never had Garcelle felt so aroused. So free. So uninhibited. So sexy. "Yes, suck them. Aahh, that feels so good," she cried out, arching her back as Kade deepened the sucking motion.

He grunted in agreement as he pressed her breasts together and suckled both of her nipples between delicious bites and licks.

Garcelle stroked his hardness until she felt the moisture drizzle from the smooth, thick tip. She felt him shiver, and his dick hardened in her grasp. "Yes, Kade," she whispered into the heated air. "Yes."

One of his large, masculine hands slid down to pet her kitty, and he pressed his fingers against her throbbing clit in a circular motion that was a mixture of torture and pleasure.

He hissed in pleasure as one of his fingers and then another slid deep into her. "Damn, it's wet," he moaned against the deep valley of her breasts.

She moved her hips against his fingers, the sounds of her wetness lightly smacking in the air. "I've never felt like this before," she admitted as she felt tiny spasms fill her core and vibrate her walls. A feeling of great excitement filled her. "I could feel like this forever."

Kade slid his fingers from her and leisurely licked

the juices from them. "It tastes as good as it smells," he told her, looking down at her as Garcelle raised her hands above her head and began to move her body as if there were music playing.

Kade stopped sucking on his fingers to watch her. Her pendulous breasts shifted to the left as her curvaceous hips moved to the right. Back and forth. Back and forth.

He felt hypnotized. He swallowed a lump in his throat.

"Hungry?" she asked as she lifted her legs above head.

Kade licked his lips. Her mound was plump and directly level with his eyes. He reached out for her hips and jerked her forward on the floor. He bent down to trace the top of his tongue against her lips, opening them slightly as he tasted her clit. He felt a shiver race through his body, and his head was clouded with desire for her.

Kade turned and lay down on his back on the floor. Following his lead, she straddled his head backwards, on her knees. He inhaled her womanly scent before he nuzzled his lips against hers. His hips arched off the floor as he felt her hands surround his hardness.

He used his hands to open her lips wide, until her small pink bud was exposed to him. The first flicker of his tongue against it made her body jump. The second flicker made her quiver. The third made her swivel her hips against his tongue.

"Yes, suck me, Kade," she hummed. "Suck me harder."

He took the bud between his lips and pulled. It swelled, and he felt her juices drizzle down his chin.

He suckled it with quick and deep motions meant to send her over the edge.

Garcelle collapsed on him, her breasts pressed against the top of his thighs, her fleshy and smooth buttocks cupping his nose as he devoured her femininity like he was starved. He reached up with one hand and lightly slapped one buttock as he pushed his tongue up into her core. Her tight, ridged walls gripped it.

He had lost the fight to resist her. He wanted nothing more than to bury himself between her heated and moist thighs.

He watched as Garcelle rose shakily to her feet and then walked into a bedroom. He jumped to his feet and followed her, but she was leaving the room before he could enter. She held up a six-pack of condoms before she grabbed his hands and led him into her own bedroom.

The red hue of her room fueled his desire as she climbed onto her bed. He climbed on behind her, and Garcelle snuggled close to him and caressed his hardness with her leg as she leaned over to lightly trace his nipple with her tongue. The soft, curly hairs of his chest tickled her tongue as the bud tightened between her lips.

Kade pushed her back against the bed and climbed between her open legs. He used one of the condoms to sheath his hardness. The tip of his shaft rested lightly between her lips as he leaned his head down to kiss her deeply. She raised her legs and wrapped them tightly around his waist, and with one thrust of his narrow hips, Kade buried his dick deep within her. He felt nothing but the warmth, the moisture, the heat, and the tightness of her center.

They both cried out. Garcelle writhed beneath him, ready for him to give her more. Kade's body was tense above hers, unable to take much more.

Slowly, once his climax subsided, he began to stroke his hardness deep inside of her until his soft hairs brushed lightly against her plump mound. He reached for her bent legs and pressed each one down on either side of her head. He winced as her walls tightened down upon him more.

Garcelle cried out and tossed her head back and forth on the pillows as she swiveled her hips and pulled down on his length.

Never had he felt so out control. "Damn," he cried out.

Kade looked down at her. Her hair was splayed across the bed. Her eyes were clouded. Her lips were slightly puffy from being well kissed. Her bronzed cheeks were slightly flushed.

Time became endless as they made love. The storm raging outside coud not compete with the passion they'd created in that small bedroom.

Kade wrapped his arms around her waist as he stroked deeply within her moist heat. Their eyes locked as they breathed in each other's essence until they both began to shiver with their rising climaxes. They brought their mouths together and kissed, clutching each other tightly and letting the tumultuous waves glide over their bodies as they gave in to losing control.

12

Kade lay on his side and looked down at Garcelle as she slept. The wall was cold against his back and buttocks, his legs and feet hung off the end of the bed, and there was hardly enough room for the two of them, but he was lying beside Garcelle, so there wasn't a better bed anywhere as far as he was concerned.

She turned on her side and snuggled against him. "Kade," she whispered in her sleep.

He bent down and kissed her bare shoulder. "I'm right here," he whispered in her ear as he placed his arm over her waist and held her close.

When Reema died, he never imagined finding a woman who would touch him as deeply ever again. He had fought his attraction and awareness of Garcelle since that first moment he saw her at Kahron's. Even then something about her shook him. He had tried to deny it, but his mind couldn't fight what his body—and his heart—wanted. Last night had been like nothing he had ever experienced. He didn't want to lose that. He didn't want to lose her. He'd had enough loss in his life.

He climbed from the bed, trying his best not to

awaken her. Naked, he walked to the living room, picked up his jeans, and slipped them on. Barefoot and shirtless, Kade checked the interior of the house to make sure there was no damage before he went outside into nothing but brilliant sunshine. The storm had come and passed. He sat down on the damp top step of the porch before he checked for any outside damage.

He was torn. He wanted to remain true to that deep and profound love he had for Reema, but he couldn't imagine his life without Garcelle. Reema was gone. She wasn't coming back. Being with Garcelle was not like having an affair. He hadn't cheated on his wife.

So why did he feel like he had?

Kade had stopped smoking back in his late twenties, but at that moment, he would have slapped a pit bull to get his hands on a cigarette.

A black car rolled into the yard. Kade squinted as the power window opened and he looked into the face of Mr. Rico Suave. Kade flexed his shoulders because there was no mistaking the anger on the other man's face.

"Is Garcelle here?" Joaquin asked as he climbed out of the car.

"She's sleeping," Kade told him as he tilted his head to the side to eye him.

"Who are you?"

"Garcelle's guest. Who are you?" Kade countered.

"Garcelle's *boyfriend*," Joaquin volleyed back, with emphasis.

Kade smiled as he squinted his eyes against the sun. "I'm pretty confident that's not true."

The man's olive complexion turned beet red in anger. "You son of a bitch!"

Kade rose to his feet as Joaquin came charging at him. He ducked a blow and followed through with a powerful uppercut, which sent Joaquin flying backwards into a puddle in the middle of the yard. When Joaquin jumped quickly to his feet and came charging at him, Kade leaped down from the porch and put his dukes up, ready to meet him head-on.

Garcelle rolled over in bed, with a deep moan of satisfaction. Stretching her limbs in the sweat-soaked and tangled sheets, she smiled at what she'd shared with Kade last night. His words. His love-making. His very presence.

She sat up. "Kade," she called out as she kicked the sheets from her legs and rose, naked, from the bed.

Was he gone? Did he regret his words? Did he regret the lovemaking? Did he regret ever coming there?

Garcelle grabbed a football jersey nightshirt and pulled it over her head as she hurried from the bedroom. She frowned at the sound of raised voices. Her eyes widened when she looked out the front door and saw Kade and Joaquin fighting on the muddy ground.

She cursed them both in Spanish as she burst out the door and leapt from the stairs, landing in a puddle and sending mud flecks and brown water splashing up onto her legs and under her short nightshirt. She raced to jump in between them. They jumped to their feet on either side of her, with their chests heaving. They were covered from head to foot in mud.

"Are you two kidding me?" she asked, looking back and forth between them. "I mean seriously. *Seriously!*"

People were out on their porches and in their yards, watching the spectacle. Garcelle could just spit in frustration at the two of them.

"Kade, go inside," she told him in a hard voice as she pointed to the door.

"Joaquin, go home," she told him as she pointed to his car.

Kade stayed still.

Joaquin's black eyes turned cold as they took in the nudeness of her body in the nightshirt, which barely covered her buttocks. "You screwing this fool while you and me are working on getting back together?"

Kade barreled toward him, and Garcelle turned and placed her hands on his chest. She could have died from embarrassment. "Go home, Joaquin. I will call you later," she called over her shoulder.

Joaquin laughed bitterly as his face twisted in anger. "What's this? Payback 'cause I dumped your ass?"

"You are a real asshole," Kade shouted as he picked Garcelle up and moved her out of his path. Kade took two long strides, then picked Joaquin up by his shirt and held him high in the air. "She said, 'Go home.'"

"How's it feel getting my leftovers?" Joaquin asked snidely as he laughed in Kade's face.

"Joaquin!" Garcelle called out sharply.

Kade turned and tossed Joaquin onto the hood of his car, with a loud thud.

The mud on his clothes sent Joaquin sliding off the hood and back into the mud. He scrambled to his feet and climbed into his car. "No need for your trickin' ass to call me. Fuck you, Garcelle," he called through his window before he reversed out of the yard, sending mud flying at Kade and Garcelle, and sped away.

Kade and Garcelle faced each other, covered from heat to foot with mud. "Would this be a spa treatment?" Garcelle asked as she used her fingers to wipe some of the mud from her face.

Kade smiled, and his white teeth showed through the mud on his own face. "I doubt it."

They started laughing together.

Garcelle moved over to him, walking with her legs spread open to keep the mud from making them stick together. She reached up to spike his hair with the mud before she placed her hands up on his shoulders. "He wasn't my boyfriend. Well, not anymore," she told him as he brought his muddy arms around her waist.

"I know that," he said.

She tilted her head back to look up at him. She smiled as he bent his head to kiss her. "Eskimo kiss," she said.

"At least the lights are on now, and we can wash," Kade said as he nuzzled the tip of his nose against hers.

In rural states like South Carolina, water was supplied by a well, and without power, the well's pump didn't work. Therefore, if there were no lights, there was no water.

"Let's go back to your house," Garcelle offered. "We can just lay around all day naked."

Kade paused. "I . . . uh, have a better idea. Kadina's gone for the weekend, and I can afford to take a mini-vacation, so let's drive into Charleston and make a weekend of it. Take in a show, get some dinner, go back to the room . . ."

"That sounds real nice, Kade," she told him, with honesty. "So nice that I might just kiss you with the mud."

"I might just let you."

"Let's go in. The neighbors have enough to talk about without me flashing them."

"After the shower, can we get a replay of last night?" he asked as he swung her up into his arms to carry her into the house.

Garcelle's smoky eyes shined through the mud as she smiled at him saucily. "After? Why not during?"

Kade walked into the house and closed the door with his foot.

Bianca tried Mimi's home number and cell phone number for the thousandth time since Mimi returned to Atlanta two weeks ago. Like always, it rang several times and then went to voice mail. She bit her bottom lip as she put her chin in her hand and looked out of the home office she shared with Kahron.

Something was definitely up with Mimi. Definitely.

She started to call Kahron, but she knew he was in horse heaven at the horse trials in Georgia. Besides, she loved her husband, and she knew that he adored her, but complications in her friendship with Mimi definitely were not uppermost in his mind . . . especially this particular weekend.

She sighed as she looked down at her schedule for the day. It was pretty much clear. Maybe she would play a little hooky herself.

She called Garcelle's house phone, but it just rang and rang. For Christmas, she was going to treat the woman to a cell phone. "Hello. It's 2007, for God's sake," Bianca muttered as she picked up the phone and dialed Kaitlyn's cell phone. Now Kaitlyn, on the other hand, didn't see the necessity of a landline phone, because she never went anywhere without her bejeweled Sidekick.

Bianca rolled her eyes as Kaitlyn's line went straight to voice mail. "I am enjoying life to the fullest, and I know you wouldn't want to disturb that, so leave me a message, and I'll get back to when my head is out of the clouds. Holla!"

"Kaitlyn. I got one word for you, heifer. Shopping. Bet that gets you out of the clouds. Call me." Bianca dropped the phone back on the hook.

Her thoughts went back to Mimi. She bit her lip and ran her fingers through her fresh straw set before she snatched up the phone to dial her father.

"King Ranch."

"Dad, uh . . . uh, have you talked to Mimi?" she asked, feeling nervous as she played with her diamond hoop earrings.

"Of course. Why? Haven't you?"

"No, I've been calling her, and she isn't answering or returning my calls."

The line went quiet.

Bianca unsnapped an earring and snapped it back on. "Okay. Spill. What's going on?"

"I'm not getting into this. You two work it out," he said gruffly.

"Work what out?" Bianca snapped.

"This is all I will say. You're my child, and I love you, but you should be more careful about what you say, because you never know who can hear you."

"Daddy, what are you talking about . . . ?"

I love my friend, but I don't think she's right for my father. The words she'd spoken in the kitchen to Garcelle came back to her. But there was no way Mimi had heard her . . . was there?

Bianca winced as she dropped her head into her hand. "Shit."

"Shit is right, Bianca."

Bianca hung up the phone. How could she fix it when Mimi wouldn't even talk to her?

Zorrie ran her hands through her hair as she slammed the phone down. Kade wasn't answering his house phone or his cell phone. "Damn, damn, damn, damn," she swore as she banged her fist against the top of her desk.

This morning she'd received a call and had to return to work. She hated that she had to cut her trip short. It couldn't be avoided if she wanted to remain the vice president of human resources for one of the largest wireless companies in the country.

She thought of the steam rising between Kade and Garcelle, and she could literally scream in frustration. She had to get back down there. She didn't give a damn if she had to fake a major illness and take long-term sick leave. She would head back to Holtsville, South Carolina, as soon as possible, and she was going to claim her ultimate prize . . . Kade Strong. She just *had* to.

"This little piggy went to the market . . . This little piggy stayed home . . . This little piggy had roast beef . . . This little piggy had none . . . And this little piggy cried, 'Wee! Wee! Wee!' all the way home."

Garcelle laughed as Kade's strong hand tickled her foot as they sat facing each other in the Jacuzzi tub filled with frothy bubbles. She tried to free her foot from his hand. "Quit, Kade. Let the little piggies go. I'm ticklish," she said, slapping her hand against the water to send some flying in his direction.

"If you get used to my touch, your feet won't be so ticklish anymore," he told her as he began to massage the soles of her feet. He laughed huskily before he wiggled his brows and then sucked her toes.

"Is that so?" Garcelle sighed, her heavily hooded eyes on him as she bit her bottom lip and gasped for breath.

"Like that?" he asked thickly as he lowered her other foot to rub up and down the length of his hard and long erection.

Garcelle panted. "*Love* . . . it."

Kade slid his hands down to her thighs and then jerked her forward until her knees were on either side of him, causing water to splash over the tub's sides to the floor. "I suddenly hate bubbles," he told her, hating that they covered her nakedness from his eyes.

Garcelle reached beneath the bubbles and drew his hands toward her, to her open core. "I don't know. Personally, I like *feeling* things even more than I like *seeing* things sometimes. You know?" she asked softly and teasingly, with a naughty laugh.

Kade palmed her intimacy. "And some things feel damn good."

"I know a hands-free way that makes some things feel even better," she said, climbing onto his lap.

"Great minds think alike."

They laughed huskily together. Then Kade reached up and drew her head down for a deep and tender kiss.

Brrrnnnggg.

Lisha and Kael exchanged an exaggerated look

at the sound of the phone ringing. Kadina lay on the floor watching her favorite Barbie DVD on the television. "If that is Zorrie again, I am going to scream," Lisha whispered to her husband as she reached for the cordless phone sitting between them on a small, round wooden table. "She's been calling all day, like she's crazy."

Brrrnnnggg.

Lisha looked at the caller ID and shook her head. "It's her."

"Don't answer it," Kael said in a calm voice as he read the local paper.

The front door opened and closed, and Kaityln breezed into the den all short skirts and high heels. "What's the deal, my people?"

Brrrnnnggg.

Kadina rolled over onto her back. "Hi, Auntie Kaitlyn."

"Hey, Li'l Diva," Kaitlyn said, bending over to tickle Kadina's tummy. Kadina burst into a fit of giggles.

Brrrnnnggg.

"Should *I* answer the phone?" Kaitlyn asked.

"Nope," Kael said as he shook the wrinkles out of the paper.

"Kaitlyn, did you get another tattoo?" Lisha asked, rising from her chair, walking over, and lifting up the back of her daughter's shirt.

Brrrnnnggg.

"Me and my girls rode to Savannah yesterday to get them. We just got back." Kaitlyn pulled down the waistband of her jean skirt to show the scroll, with her name in the middle, at the base of her spine.

Lisha's face was filled with disapproval. "You know,

if you have kids, you can't give them blood, because of those things."

Brrrnnnggg.

"Speaking of kids . . . I've been dreaming about fish," said Lisha as she gave her rambunctious daughter a hard stare.

"Don't look at me," Kaitlyn immediately protested.

It was an old wives' tale in the South that when someone dreamt of fish, someone in their family was pregnant.

Brrrnnnggg.

"Kael, remember the last time I dreamt of fish, our little grandbaby over there came seven months later," said Lisha.

"Sure did," replied Kael.

Lisha eyed her daughter again.

Brrrnnnggg.

"Who is that, and why won't they hang up?" Kaitlyn asked suddenly, moving over to snatch up the phone.

"Somebody who obviously don't have a bit of good common sense," Kael drawled as he shifted his reading glasses.

"Hello," Kaitlyn said, with more than a little attitude.

"Kaitlyn? Hey. This is Zorrie."

"Zorrie, listen. Uh, you know, usually when I call someone's house and they don't answer after a few rings, I hang up. You know what I'm saying?"

Kael grunted.

"I wanted to check on Kade after the storm. That's all," Zorrie said defensively.

Kaitlyn reached in her Juicy Couture bag for a stick of gum. "Well, Kade is not here, and he will not be coming here anytime tonight, okay?" Kaitlyn made a face like "What don't you understand?"

"I've been calling his cell phone, and he isn't answering, so I was worried—"

"I just spoke to him about an hour ago," said Kaitlyn. "He's fine. The house is fine. Kadina is fine. We're all fine. So if he's not answering for *you*, then he doesn't want to speak to *you*."

Lisha reached up and snatched the phone from her daughter. "Zorrie, this is Mrs. Strong. Next time we speak to Kade, we'll let him know you're trying to reach him, okay?"

"Now see. I thought y'all wanted it handled, so I handled it," Kaitlyn said. "Right, Pops?"

"All the time. All the time," said Kael.

Lisha hung up the phone. "Stop being so rude to people, Kaitlyn."

Kaitlyn kicked off her shoes and dropped down on the floor, next to her niece. "Rude is calling someone's house and letting the phone ring a gazillion times like you're going to *make* them answer their phone."

Lisha nudged her daughter's backside with her foot. "You answer your phone at your house the way you want."

"Grandma, can I have a snack?" Kadina asked.

"Yeah, and bring me one," Kael said, stepping in.

Kadina went running from the room.

"Why is she semi-stalking Kade, anyway?" Kaitlyn asked.

Lisha shrugged. "She was just concerned. You know, they've been friends since high school."

"Some friend," Kaitlyn muttered. "I hope none of my girls put the moves—no matter how slick—on my husband after I'm dead."

* * *

Garcelle released a nervous breath and smiled at her reflection as she stood in the bathroom of their hotel suite in downtown Charleston. She was happy.

Completely and blissfully happy.

They hadn't left the suite all day. Not to eat or to sightsee or to shop. It had been a Kade and Garcelle fest.

They made love. Talked about their childhoods. Ordered room service. Made love some more. Took a bubble bath. Flirted. Made love some more. Watched television. Shared stories about Kadina. Made love some more. And some more. And some more.

The man's appetite for sex was voracious. He was definitely making up for his celibacy. She shivered at the fierceness of his delivery. Each and every time he was as hard as jail time.

They were finally venturing out for dinner, and she wanted everything to be perfect. She leaned forward in the mirror and double-checked her makeup. Her complexion had never been so vibrant.

As she opened the bathroom door, she took a deep breath and hoped that she wouldn't regret crossing that line with Kade. She didn't want to be hurt.

Kade turned away from the night view of the Charleston skyline. He looked handsome in his navy tailored suit, with a simple but classic white shirt. His hair was still damp from his shower and was brushed back from his square and handsome face. All of it made his eyes so much more intense as he stared at her.

Garcelle had taken her time to curl her hair, and her make-up was dramatic, with smoky eyes and a clear lip gloss on her lips. The white dress she wore hugged her small breasts before falling to an empire

waist and stopping mid-thigh, showing off her
shapely and thick legs. Four-inch rhinestone sandals
actually brought her closer to his height and worked
with the length of the dress to showcase her legs.

This was a Garcelle she rarely took the time to
display.

"Wow," he said, as if she truly took his breath away.

13

Bianca arrived in Atlanta in just under four hours. As she parked in front of Mimi's mini-mansion in the exclusive gated community where she had once owned a home, she struggled to get her words together. Climbing out of the car, she grabbed her overnight bag.

Because the guards at the gate had alerted Mimi to her presence, she already stood in the open doorway. She was dressed in pale pink slacks and a silk shirt. Her face was like stone as she looked at Bianca as if she were a stranger.

"Are you going to let me in, or did I just drive from Holtsville for nothing?" said Bianca.

"I love your father, Bianca," Mimi said in a hard voice.

"I know you do," Bianca answered honestly.

"I wouldn't do anything to hurt him," said Mimi, with tears rising in her eyes.

Bianca stepped up and squeezed her hand. "Mimi, do we have to do this in your doorway? Can I come in?"

Mimi looked anything but happy about stepping

back and allowing Bianca to walk into her home. "You really hurt my feelings, Bianca," she said before Bianca even reached the stark white leather and mink living room. "And only people I care about can hurt me."

"I'm sorry. I love you to death, but to be honest, with my father's drinking problem and *your* drinking problem, I worried it was like adding kerosene to a fire."

Mimi sauntered across the floor in her heels and moved over to the bar. "*My* drinking problem?" she asked as she dropped ice cubes in a glass.

Bianca fell back against the white leather sofa in exasperation. "Mimi, are you fixing . . . a . . . *drink*?"

"For you, because *you* do still drink, don't you?" Mimi walked over and handed the glass to Bianca.

Bianca accepted it but sat it on the white leather ottoman. "Mimi—"

Mimi moved to the foyer and came back with a pale pink Gucci purse. She reached over the back of the sofa to give it to Bianca. "Hold on to that. I'll be right back," she said over her shoulder as she climbed the gold circular staircase.

"Mimi—"

"Be right back," Mimi sang down to Bianca.

For the next ten minutes, Bianca walked every inch of the living room. She even played around on the white baby grand piano in the corner.

"Bianca, meet Beulah Cooley."

Bianca looked up, and her fingers hit the wrong piano keys when she beheld Mimi sans make-up and high hair, and with the normal voice . . . like she was at the cookout.

"Mimi, what the hell is going on with you, and who the hell is Beulah?" Bianca eyed her warily. "Am

I going to have to knock you out with a two-by-four and run for my life? 'Cause you got my ass scared right now."

Mimi rolled her eyes before she turned and scooped up her purse, from which she removed her silver monogrammed flask. She walked back over to Bianca and handed the flask to her. "Have some?"

Bianca shook her head. "No thanks. I would tell you to sip away, but I think you've had enough—"

"It's sweet tea."

Bianca snorted. "Yeah, right."

Mimi stuck it under her nose.

Bianca sniffed and then snatched the flask to taste its contents. "Oh my God, it *is* tea!"

Mimi's face was all "I told you so."

"Mimi, okay. What is your point?" Bianca asked.

Mimi sat on the sofa as she waved her hand at her lavish home. "This is all I've known. Since I was a child actor, everything about me and my life has been over the top. And the only thing I know how to do is act. Can you imagine being fresh in your twenties and realizing no one in Hollywood cares anymore? But this is the only life I know how to live, and it's not me. Well, it's not all me. I mean, who wouldn't love Manolos?"

Bianca walked over to the ottoman and picked up her drink. "Lucy, you gots some explaining to do," she told Mimi in a bad Ricky Ricardo accent before she tossed the drink back.

"I thought I just explained," Mimi said calmly.

"So the drinking, the makeup, the Diahann Carroll wardrobe, *that damned accent* . . . it's all been what? An act?"

"Self entertainment. Fun. I mean, come on.

Everyone loves Mimi. Mimi can say what she wants and do what she wants, and nobody lifts a brow. I loved it. I thrived on this grand act, but now I'm real interested in life on a ranch in Holtsville, South Carolina, and I know all of this can't fit there."

Bianca leaned back against the chair as she looked over at Mimi. "And you would give all of this up for my father?" she asked as she waved her hand around the house and then at Mimi, from head to foot.

"In a heartbeat."

Bianca rose to her feet and opened her arms. "Then welcome to the family, you nut case," she said lovingly as she embraced Mimi tightly.

Zorrie hated that Kade wasn't answering her calls. And then his sister had given her all that attitude on the phone. She just felt like something was wrong. She *had* to talk to Kade.

She hopped into her Benz and headed to South Carolina. She didn't pack a bag. She didn't notice that her fuel light had come on until she reached Florence, South Carolina. She fueled up and hopped back onto Interstate 95.

The entire time she drove, she alternated between calling Kade's cell phone and his house phone. She received no answer on either. She had nearly bitten her nails down to the nub by the time she pulled into Kade's yard.

His vehicle wasn't there, and he never parked in the garage. Besides, all the lights were off, so she knew he wasn't home. "I'll just wait," she said as she shut her car off.

* * *

Although they had spent the entire weekend together, Garcelle still felt disappointed when they made the turn down the unpaved road leading to his house. She had driven her car to Kade's and had left it in his garage before they headed to Charleston.

"Are you going to pick up Kadina today, or should I pick her up in the morning, on my way to work?" Garcelle asked as she turned her head on the headrest to look at him.

"I'll get her. They're probably just getting out of church," he said, picking up their entwined hands to kiss hers.

Garcelle smiled at him before she turned her head back as his house came into sight. She looked confused at the sight of a car parked there. "Is that Zorrie's car? Is she back in town?"

Kade frowned as he released Garcelle's hand and steered the vehicle to a stop next to the Benz. "Is she in there?" he asked incredulously.

Garcelle rose up in her seat and could hardly believe the sight of Zorrie, who was sleeping on her side on the car seat, reclined all the way back. "That *puta* is *muy loca*," Garcelle said as she looked at Kade.

"Has she been there all night?"

"Kade, please wake up. *Please*," Garcelle said, with emphasis, as she made a fist and lightly knocked on his head. "She has been calling you like crazy all weekend and wouldn't leave a voice mail, because she knows she didn't want a dang thing. You said your sister called and said Zorrie was phone stalking you via your parents' phone line. Now here she is. She likes you. She wants you. She wants to make nasty with you and bad."

"We're just friends. . . ."

Garcelle threw her hands up and let out a string

of Spanish expletives as she climbed from the SUV. "Kade, handle it. Your wife's best friend just slept outside your house all night. Shit, man. *Handle* it."

She slammed the passenger door and quickly strode toward the back of the house. She had to fight the urge to shake the car and rattle Zorrie from her sleep. She didn't give Kade another look as she walked around the back of the house to the garage.

Garcelle laid on her horn as she passed Zorrie's car. She laughed when the woman sat straight up in the seat and got tangled in the seat belt. That gave her a good laugh all the way home.

At first I thought Aunt Zorrie was here to see me, but I think she just wants to see you.

If a man and a woman go out to eat, to the movies, and all that good stuff . . . they are dating, baby . . . That woman is a barracuda in disguise. . . .

Look here, big brother. Take it from a woman. Zorrie got an agenda. Sleep on her if you want to.

Kade, please wake up. Please.

Kade climbed from the SUV as all the phrases came floating back to him. Was he naïve to think Zorrie wanted nothing but the friendship he had to offer her? She was Reema's best friend. She wouldn't want to betray Reema like that and certainly didn't think he would ever consider doing such a thing. Did she?

He walked around to open her car door. "Zorrie, what are you doing here?" he asked.

She wiped the dried drool from the corners of her mouth as she climbed out of the car, clearly disheveled and wrinkled from sleeping in a car all night.

"Was that Garcelle that just left here?" she asked.

He released a heavy breath. "Zorrie, why are you sleeping outside my house, ringing my parents' phone off the hook, and damn near making my cell phone battery go dead from calling me?"

She placed her tousled hair behind her ears. "I was worried about you after the storm, and after I couldn't reach you, I wanted to make sure you and Kadina were okay."

"So you drove from North Carolina and slept outside my house?" he asked.

"Kade, I was so worried, and if you had just answered my call . . ."

"Garcelle and I spent the weekend together, and when you didn't leave a voice mail, I figured whatever you had to tell me could wait until our weekend was over."

He was surprised by the flash of anger in her eyes.

"Garcelle?" she spat. "So, what? You fucking her?"

He was shocked by the vulgarity of Zorrie's words. Miss Prim and Proper never cursed. Ever.

"No, I'm dating her," he responded calmly as he began to feel uncomfortable in Zorrie's presence.

"So you feel a lazy, wetback nanny is good enough to replace *my* best friend?"

Distaste filled him. "You know, I would've thought you were too smart and too classy to use racial slurs, especially since you're a minority woman."

"Don't you dare stand in my face and judge me!"

He frowned at the intensity of her anger. "What? Garcelle's not good enough, but you are? Right?"

"You're damn right I'm good enough. I'm better than good enough. I'm the one you should have chosen in the first damn place—"

She slapped her hands over her own mouth.

Kade leaned against the hood of her car as he

crossed his arms over his chest. "Zorrie, I picked Reema because I liked her. I married her because I loved her. And I would never date her best friend, because I respect her."

Zorrie ran her shaking hands through her hair as she walked away from him. Then she walked back, with tears in her eyes. "Kade, I—"

He held up his hands. "Zorrie, I consider you a good friend. A lot has been said. Some of it can't be taken back. Let's not say anything else to make this situation any worse than it is."

She nodded and released a shaky breath as she crossed her arms over her chest and paced in front of him. She stopped and faced him, with tears and pain in her eyes. "That day when Reema and I sat there together in the cafeteria, side by side, you walked up and your eyes went straight to her. Why didn't you see *me*? Why didn't you look over at *me*?"

He felt sorry for her. The woman was deeply wounded, and he knew there was more to it than just him. "I don't know why, Zorrie. And it doesn't matter, because I wouldn't change a thing if I had the chance."

She stared at him a long time before she sniffed back her tears. "I think it would be best if I just go, and maybe I . . . maybe we . . . should give each other some space."

Kade stood up. "You want me to drive you somewhere?"

She shook her head as she opened her car door. "It's time I learned to live without you," she told him before she climbed into the vehicle and reversed out of the yard.

* * *

Garcelle was lying across her bed, on her stomach, reading when there was a knock at her door. She looked over her shoulder to see her little brother, Paco, peek his head inside.

"You awake? Uncle Anthony said you had a call on the other line," said Paco.

"Bring it to me," she said as she turned over and sat up in bed.

Paco brushed his long bangs out of his eyes as he walked into Garcelle's room, with the phone outstretched in his hands. "Uncle Anthony said to hurry up. He's on the other line."

"Surprise, surprise," Garcelle said as she pressed the phone to her ear. "Hello?"

"Garcelle. This is me. You busy?" said Kade.

She felt her body go warm at the sound of Kade's voice. "Hold on one sec."

She clicked the phone and got the other line. "Anthony said he'll call you back," she said, without waiting for an answer. She clicked back over.

Paco was snooping around her dresser. "Tell Uncle Anthony he'll have to call them back. Now come here," said Garcelle.

He walked over to her, and she kissed her two fingers before she pressed them to his forehead. "Good night, Paco."

"Night."

She waited until he had closed the door behind him before she turned out the light and snuggled down under the sheets on her bed. "Okay. I'm back."

"Good," said Kade.

"Where's Kadina?" she asked as she crossed one leg over the other.

"I just put her to bed. She's been grilling me all day about my weekend."

"I don't think there's too much about this weekend that was G-rated."

Kade laughed huskily. "Me either."

They fell into a comfortable silence just listening to each other breathe.

14

Six Weeks Later

Garcelle pushed her shades on top of her hair as she leaned against the wooden fence and looked out at Kadina astride a horse, being led around a paddock. In truth, a small girl riding a horse made her nervous, and she didn't have the same enthusiasm Kade had for Kadina learning to ride. Just over two months ago, he'd bruised his own ribs from a hard tumble off a horse, which could've ended much worse. She was learning that the Strongs considered riding a horse as normal as breathing air or walking upright.

"Look, Garcelle, look," Kadina called out to her.

Garcelle clapped her hands as the ranch hand took the horse from a trot to a gallop. "I'm looking," she called back. *And praying*, she added silently.

Unlike other members of her family, Garcelle had never ridden a horse, and she wasn't looking to change that fact anytime soon. She just felt good lounging outside in the sun as she watched Kadina closely to make sure she was safe.

Garcelle's butt began to vibrate, and she reached into her back pocket for her new cell phone. Kade had insisted she get one, especially when he discovered just how much time her uncles spent on the house phone at night. A couple of nights of not being able to reach her, and he presented her with the gift of the phone.

"Hello," she said into the phone as she dropped her shades back down onto her face.

"I was riding by and saw this sexy Latina. I just had to ask her name."

Garcelle frowned. She recognized Kade's voice, but she was willing to play along. "It's Garcelle. Garcelle Santos. And you are?" she asked as she twirled around to look for him.

"A secret admirer."

She smiled. "Oh, well, I thank you for that, but I only recognize a man who can stand up like a man and let a woman know how he feels."

"I wanted to see if you had a man in your life first."

"Oh." Her eyes darted everywhere, but she didn't see him, and he had to be around. "I don't know if I like a man who worries about the next man before he worries about his interest in me."

"So you do have a man?"

Garcelle turned and leaned her back against the fence. "Oh yes, but he's like an old man," she said very tongue in cheek. "He already has silver hair, and soon he'll need Viagra to keep up with me—"

"Garcelle!"

"Yes, Kade," she answered in a simple tone.

She heard the hooves pounding against the ground before she saw him racing toward her from the top of the hill. She closed her phone as he galloped around the paddock and approached her.

"Viagra," he stressed as he looked down at her, with a scowl.

Garcelle smiled up at him, with flashing eyes filled with laughter. "Ooh, poor baby," she cooed as she reached up to pat his thigh. "He likes to play on the phone but can't take someone playing with him."

His eyes dropped down to her hand high on his thigh. "Oh, I can take you playing with me," he told her thickly.

Garcelle saw his rod stir to life in his pants, and she felt her entire body warm over as she shifted her gaze up to meet his. "See. You are a dirty old man," she teased, with a husky voice.

"If I'm so dirty, then I need to clean off." He licked his lip a little before he smiled like a rogue. "Know something wet I can get into?"

Garcelle's mouth formed a circle. "Oooh, you are *so* bad."

"Come ride with me, Daddy," Kadina called out to him from the paddock.

With a lot of reluctance, they broke their hot stare at one another.

Garcelle frowned as Kade held his hand out to her. Kade laughed. "Come on. Ride with me."

She shook her head. "Who me? Oh no. Garcelle don't do horses."

The ranch hand brought Kadina's horse to a stop behind them. "Garcelle doesn't ride, Daddy," Kadina offered, with a giggle.

Kade's hand remained outstretched. "Come on. I'll teach you."

"Please, Garcelle," Kadina whined behind her.

Garcelle looked at Kadina quickly over her shoulder before she turned back to look up at Kade. A blind man could see she was hesitant.

"Trust me. No horse racing," he joked.

"That's good to know," Garcelle muttered before she took a deep breath and put her hand in his.

As soon as she was settled in the saddle, in front of Kade, he wrapped his arm lightly around her waist. "Kade, nice and slow, okay?" she warned him as he steered the horse around and entered the paddock.

He chuckled. "Oh, I know you like it nice and slow, Garcelle," he reminded her warmly in her ear.

"You're acting like a horny little boy," she scolded him playfully.

"First a dirty old man and now a horny little boy?" Garcelle bit back a smile. "*Sí.*"

"Why not just a grown-ass man who finds a grown-ass woman sexy as hell?"

At the sound of his low and erotic tone, Garcelle shivered and had to force herself not to turn around and see if it was possible to ride him in the saddle.

"People are watching, Kade, so stop being fresh."

He just laughed as he kicked the horse's flanks to trot around the paddock.

"You okay?" he asked.

Garcelle's buttocks were pressed against the top of Kade's thighs, giving her a rather intimate feel of his hardness. "The horse is fine. It's you that's making me nervous. Kade, you're *hard.*"

"Now who's being fresh?" he teased.

Each jostle of the horse brought her buttocks slightly up and then against his steely hardness. That, plus the natural heat of his body, made her forget the damn horse.

"In one of my first dreams of making love to you, we were in the big field, on horseback," he whispered near her ear.

Garcelle's eyes widened as she turned slightly to look at him over her shoulder. "No," she said in shock.

"Yeah."

"I dreamt the same thing."

Now it was Kade's turn to fill with surprise. "No."

"Yes," she told him, with emphasis.

They both looked away, a bit pensive, before their eyes shifted back to each other. "We couldn't," they said in unison.

Garcelle turned back around as Kade steered their horse up beside Kadina's horse.

"See, Garcelle. It's fun, right?" asked Kadina.

Garcelle forced a smile. "Yes, I'm having a ball," she told her. *And the bat*, she thought, with a chuckle, as her bottom again rose and fell against his hardness.

It had been a little over a week since they'd had any time alone, and this impromptu horseback ride was really making that hit home for Garcelle. She missed him. During the day, she watched over Kadina, and he worked. At night he watched over Kadina, and she was home.

Kade motioned for the ranch hand to pass him the reins to Kadina's horse.

"Where we going, Daddy?" Kadina asked as Kade led her horse out of the paddock.

"You're going to the house to sit with Grandma while Garcelle and I ride for a little," replied Kade.

Garcelle looked over her shoulder at him in surprise. "We are?" she asked, with a lift of her brow.

"I wanna go, Daddy," Kadina said.

"Next time, baby girl. I want to show Garcelle the ranch," he said, his voice stern.

Garcelle was surprised when Kadina offered no further argument. She had her father wrapped around her finger and knew it. Garcelle did not doubt that Kadina could get Kade to do whatever she wanted. Luckily, she used her powers over her father for good. *She's a good kid.*

They rode together across the ranch, toward the big house. They moved across the couple hundred yards pretty slowly, and Garcelle was sure Kade took his time as a way to appease Kadina after not allowing her to go along for their ride. *He's a good father.*

Garcelle actually felt herself relax in the saddle.

"What's black and white and red all over?" Kadina asked them as she braided her horse's jet-black hair.

"What's black and white and red all over?" Kade said slowly as if pondering the question. "Let's see. . . ."

"Daddy, this is *so* easy." Kadina rolled her eyes playfully.

"A zebra with ketchup poured all over it?" asked Kade.

"Nope."

"A panda bear soaked in cherry Kool-Aid?"

"No . . . no . . . no."

"A cow that fell in tomato soup?"

"*Dad-dy.*"

Garcelle smiled at their lighthearted exchange as they trotted up a small incline. The rays of the sun suddenly intensified, and she dropped her shades back down over her eyes.

"It's a newspaper, Daddy," Kadina drawled.

Kade snapped his finger. "Damn, I was just about to say that."

"Do you believe that, Garcelle?" Kadina asked her.

"I plead the fifth," said Garcelle.

Kadina scrunched up her face. "Huh?"

Kade and Garcelle laughed.

They reached the house, and Garcelle's eyes widened when Kade pressed the reins into her hands before he got down off the horse. "You're not leaving me up here by myself," she screeched as he did just that.

He laughed.

"Kade . . . *Kade* . . . Kade!" cried Garcelle.

He tied the reins to Kadina's horse to the long rail running across the left side of the house.

Garcelle cursed him under her breath in Spanish, and he laughed some more as he put his hands on Kadina's waist to help her down off the horse. She prayed her horse didn't decide to go for a run, because she'd be screwed.

"Bye, Daddy. Bye, Garcelle," Kadina hollered to them as she raced up the stairs. She reached the top and turned to look down at them as she cocked her head to the side. "Now don't y'all do anything I wouldn't do."

With that said, she turned and walked into the house before they could even respond. "What am I going to do with her?" Kade asked as he climbed back into the saddle, behind Garcelle, and took the reins from her.

"I have no idea."

"I know what I'm going to do with you," he whispered in her ear.

Garcelle moaned, with an exaggerated shiver.

Kade laughed as he steered the horse back across the ranch. "There's about a thousand acres of this property," he told her as he settled his arm around her waist. "Growing up, I felt the world began and ended on this ranch. If it wasn't for school, we probably would have never left it. Everything was right here."

Garcelle listened to him as she let her hands rest lightly on top of his thighs.

"Ah man, there's nothing better than skinny-dipping in a cool pond on a hot summer day or playing hardball in a big, open field where trees can be your bases."

"Sounds like you had a wonderful childhood, Kade," Garcelle told him softly.

"I remember one time my brothers and I went on strike from working the ranch, and uh . . . we ran away. We stayed right here, on the property. Just as stupid." He laughed at the memory.

"With a thousand acres, I guess it took your father a long while to find his little boys."

Kade snorted. "My father? Shoot, he left our asses right out there. We lasted about six hours, until that sun went down and that cold starting nipping at us. Kaeden caught a cold just that quick. We were hungry 'cause I ate all the snacks we brought. Wasn't nothing to do but admit defeat and stupidity while we walked back home. Then, when we did get back, he had the door locked, talking 'bout how once we move out, there's no moving back in."

"Aww, poor babies," Garcelle teased.

"Oh, my father was definitely in a Bill Cosby type of fathering mode."

"Did any of you run away again?"

"Six hours in the woods and two hours on the porch before Mama made Daddy let us back in? Shit. Trust me, that was the first *and* the last time."

Garcelle laughed as she relaxed against Kade's strong chest. "I would run away with you anytime, Kade Strong."

Kade steered the horse past the busy ranch hands, whose eyes drifted to them in open curiosity.

"Where would you go with me? Jamaica? Back to the Dominican Republic?" he asked warmly as they rode until they were surrounded by nothing but long stretches of cleared, flat land, which was obviously used for grazing.

Garcelle bit her bottom lip as she shook her head slowly. "If I could close my eyes and make a wish to go anywhere with you in the world, I would find that cool pond you all used to skinny-dip in," she told him, with honesty.

"Hold on."

Garcelle shrieked as the horse suddenly tore off at a full run across the open plain. "Kade . . . *Kade* . . . Kade!"

"Just hold on, baby. Hold on."

She shut her eyes and opened her mouth as he steered the horse near a wide road between two groves of trees.

She didn't open her eyes again or stop praying until he brought the horse to a complete stop. Her body relaxed against him, and she let out a very deep and very shaky breath.

"You okay?" he asked.

She nodded.

"So open your eyes."

Garcelle did, and she gasped at the lush green grass and flowers surrounding a small, circular pond.

"Your wish is my command," Kade told her as he slid one of his hands under her T-shirt. She gasped as his hand massaged the full globe before his warm and deliciously calloused fingers teased and tweaked her nipple. "So you want to get naked with me?" he asked her thickly as his hardening length pressed against the plush softness of her buttocks.

Garcelle leaned slightly to the left and tilted her

head back to look up into his eyes. "I always hate having clothes on around you," she whispered against his lips before she gave him a coy smile.

"I can't get enough of you." Kade moaned in the back of his throat as he pressed his lips against her open and waiting mouth.

She felt a shiver race across his body as she suckled his tongue gently in her mouth before she lightly flicked the tip of her tongue against his own.

"Nice trick," he told her, with a smile.

"You like?" she asked saucily.

"I like. I like."

Garcelle lifted her leg up and sat sidesaddle, and then she brought her other leg around to straddle the saddle, facing Kade. She smiled, with a slight tilt of her head, as she lightly grabbed the lapels of his uniform shirt. "This isn't that comfortable, *but* looking up into that gorgeous face of yours makes the pain in my ass and thighs worthwhile."

Kade laughed, and his face was transformed: his eyes brightened, and his white, straight teeth flashed against the smooth bronze of his skin. He used his hands to lift her legs so that they were settled on top of his. "Better?" he asked.

"Much," she said, with emphasis. "Have you ridden with a lady in your saddle before, cowboy?"

Kade shook his head as he looked down into her eyes.

She playfully wiggled her brows as she brought her hands down to the front of his shirt. "You have about a million of these shirts, right?" she asked coyly.

"I wouldn't say a million, but I have a lot—"

"So you won't mind me doing this?" Garcelle tore the shirt open, and the buttons flew, exposing his chiseled chest, lightly covered with soft and flat silver hairs. She lowered her head and circled one of his nipples with her very clever tongue.

Kade swallowed a lump in his throat. "Nope. I . . . uh . . . I don't mind at all."

Garcelle gave his nipple one last rollover with her tongue before she sat up straight, pulled her T-shirt over her head, and flung it over her head. Her bra followed next. She enjoyed the warmth of Kade's eyes on her as she gave her free breasts a little shimmy and shake. "Last one in sucks big time," she told him playfully.

She lifted her leg back over to sit sidesaddle before she jumped down to the ground to continue stripping off her clothes.

"Depending on what I have to suck, I might like to lose this one."

Garcelle flung her lace panties up to him with a flick of her foot. "That's the same thing I was thinking."

Kade pressed her lingerie closer to his face to inhale deeply of her scent before he dismounted the horse and tied its reins to a bush. He stared at her as he removed his clothes and boots.

Garcelle bit the side of her index finger as she watched Kade stride around in the buff like he knew just how damn good his body looked to her. Defined muscles other men dreamed of and most women wanted flexed as he reached into the saddlebag for a blanket. Wide shoulders. Strong back. Square buttocks. Toned thighs. Killer calves.

And then he turned and stepped toward her. She swallowed hard as her eyes went back to work. Solid chest. Defined, rock-hard abs. Impressive . . . lengthy . . . solid . . . pleasuring . . . hard.

"Don't stare. It might drop off," Kade teased.

Her eyes jumped up from his crotch to his face before she stepped forward, pressed the length of her body against his, and snaked her arms around his neck.

Kade brought his hands up to cup her buttocks as Garcelle planted smooth kisses along his collarbone. "I thought you wanted to cool off?" he said.

"Later. Right now I like being hot," Garcelle whispered.

Kade kissed her deeply as they lowered their bodies to the plush blades of grass. Garcelle opened her legs wide for him as he settled his muscled frame atop her body. Soon their mingled cries of fiery passion drifted high up to the skies.

Kade massaged Garcelle's lower back as she lay atop his body. He felt her heart beating against his rib cage. He enjoyed the steady in and out of her breathing. He cherished the feeling of her body against his. "To think we . . . uh . . . thought this watering hole was only good for swimming," he mused as he placed one arm under his head on the blanket.

Garcelle lifted her head from his chest to look up at him, with a soft smile. "Which memory will you treasure more? Making love here or swimming here?"

Kade caressed her face with his eyes. "Why not make a whole new memory?"

"What's that?"

"Make love *while* swimming."

Garcelle looked contemplative before she suddenly jumped to her feet. "The bet is still on, you know," she told him as she nudged his foot with her own.

Kade looked up at her body, framed by sunlight, and he swore he'd never seen a more beautiful sight than her caramel skin, softly rounded shoulders, small but plump breasts, and deeply curved hips, with the most divine set of legs God ever blessed a woman with. She playfully stuck out her tongue at him before she tossed her hair from her face and turned to run and jump headfirst into the water.

He loved her spirit. Her spunk. Her fire. Her passion. She wore her emotions on her sleeve. Be it anger, pleasure, happiness, sadness, or desire, there was no mistaking what Garcelle felt. Nothing was hidden. Nothing at all.

Kade jumped to his feet and dived into the water behind her. It felt like cool silk wrapped around his body, from his head to his toes. He opened his eyes under the water and caught the image of Garcelle's nude body as she swam to the top. He doubted there was a more magical sight than that.

He swam toward her and wrapped his arms around her as they broke the surface of the water together. The water plastered their hair against their heads. They took deep breaths and looked at each other. His heart surged as he kissed her, and they moved their bodies backward. The water intensified the already smooth feel of her body as she wrapped her legs around his waist. He pressed her against the bank, and her hands came up to rest lightly on his shoulders.

"Garcelle," he moaned against her lips and then her cheeks.

"Yes," Garcelle whispered, with a small gasp, which let him know that everything he did was just right.

He kissed her chin.

"Yes."

Her neck.

"Yes, Kade. Yes."

Her shoulders . . . from the left to the right.

"Yes."

Her collarbone.

"Umm."

Her lips again.

"Oh."

And again.

"Ooh."

And again.

"Kade."

And again.

"*Kade.*"

He deepened the kiss as the temperature of the water seemed to change from the heat of their bodies. "Garcelle, we used the condoms I had. I'm all out."

She dropped her head on his shoulder . . . several times.

He chuckled as he pressed the side of his face against hers. "Come on. I have to get back, anyway," he said, with obvious regret.

Garcelle lifted her body up onto the edge of the bank. She bent her legs in front of him. Kade's eyes smoldered as he moved forward in the water. At the water's edge, he kissed Garcelle, blazing a trail from her knee to her core. Garcelle stood up quickly and then pressed her foot to his forehead and sent him flying backwards into the water. "We have to go, remember?" she teased as she raced around the small pond to their pile of discarded clothing.

She was bending over, drying her legs off with the blanket, when Kade walked up to her. He slapped her bottom soundly with his palm before he reached into the saddlebag for another rolled-up blanket.

They eyed each other mischievously as they finished getting dressed.

"So swimming or making love?" she asked him in a breathy voice as she dropped down to the ground to pull on her socks and sneakers.

Kade wiped his hands over his mouth before he stepped forward to help her to her feet. He immediately pulled her body against his and bent his head to nuzzle her neck. "Definitely making love."

Garcelle laughed.

He helped her climb onto the saddle before he untied the horse and climbed on behind her. "Ready to head back to the real world?" he asked as he turned the horse around.

Garcelle turned and gave the pond one last look before she glanced up at Kade. She nodded. With one final kiss, she turned back around in the saddle. "I wish we could have a picnic right here."

"We can come back another day."

"Promise?" she asked.

Kade settled his hand lightly around her waist. "I promise."

In just another week, her position as Kadina's nanny would end for the summer as Kadina returned to school and Garcelle resumed her university classes. Of course, the end of the summer position didn't mean the end of their relationship, but he felt saddened by it, anyway. He was going to miss her presence around the house.

They rode in comfortable silence through the emerald green lands and towering trees to the uncluttered and open plains before the noises of the ranch began to reach them.

Kade allowed himself one last sniff of her hair as he trotted through the ranch to the main house. He dismounted, then helped Garcelle down off the horse, with regret. Even after three hours of being with her, he already missed her. So quickly, she had become so important to his life. He wished for the comfort and ease of being able to offer his woman a kiss as they parted, but he just stepped back from her

Kadina raced out onto the porch to meet them. His mother and sister followed at a slower pace. "I thought y'all wasn't ever coming back," Kadina said, moving down the steps to throw her arm around Garcelle's waist.

"I was showing Garcelle the ranch," Kade said, climbing back into the saddle.

Kaitlyn and his mother shared a brief look before they both murmured, "Uh-huh," with obvious disbelief.

"Kadina, let's get ready to go," Garcelle said, ignoring the women's teasing smiles. "We still have to go by Uncle Kahron's, remember?"

"Bye, Nana. Bye, Auntie," Kadina hollered over her shoulder before she climbed into the back of Garcelle's convertible.

"Bye, everyone," said Garcelle. She gave Kade one last look and a half smile before she climbed into the driver's seat and reversed in a semicircle, then accelerated down the driveway.

Kade waved as Kadina turned in her seat. "Don't be late, Daddy," she called to him.

"Big brother, there's nothing *that* interesting around this ranch that takes three hours to show anybody," Kaitlyn said, very tongue in cheek. "What on earth were you two doing?"

"Yes, son," Lisha added. "Your father called looking for you. He said one of the calves is about to foal—"

Kade tipped his baseball cap to them. "Then,

ladies, I better get back to work." He smiled as soon as his back was turned to them.

"I been dreaming about fish, Kade," his mother called behind him.

"It's not me, Ma," he called back over his shoulder as he trotted away.

15

One Week Later

Kahron and Bianca laughed as her stomach growled quite loudly. It seemed to echo in the interior of his vintage Mustang. "Hungry, baby?" he asked her as he reached over to squeeze her thigh.

"Starving," she answered, with emphasis. "I begged your daddy to make me some okra stew. I am dying for some good okra stew."

"I'm dying to know what their big news is." Kahron eased the car around the turn leading to his parents' home. "And if it's about her fish dreams, I'm going to scream."

"Oh my God. Your mother has called me every day for the last week, talking about fish *and* babies *and* prenatal vitamins!" Bianca covered her face with her hands. "Yes, I don't want to hear nothing 'bout birthin' no babies."

Kahron laughed as he pulled the car to a stop in between Kade's SUV and Kaeden's silver Mercedes Benz. "She is hell-bent and determined that there is another grand on the way."

"Well, it's not us," Bianca said as they climbed out of the low-slung car.

"Not yet, anyway," Kahron added. "But soon."

Bianca looked at him as he jogged up the stairs. "Real . . . soon?" she asked in surprise.

Kahron turned, his face framed by the porch light as he looked down at her. "Hell, yeah. Right?"

She smiled as she nodded and slipped her hand into his. "Right."

Kade looked up from watching a sports news show on the television as Kahron and Bianca walked into the house together. His brother hugged his wife close to his side before he kissed her forehead as they greeted everyone.

Kade literally ached for Garcelle to be there with him. She *should* have been there with him. They had plans to meet up and go to the movies later, but right now he missed her there with him, enjoying the fun and craziness of his big family. Just being close to him.

He just didn't know if he was ready to inform the world about his business. For so long, his family and friends had worried him about getting back into the dating game. As soon as they knew about Garcelle, it would be all about marriage and more babies. Hell, his momma was already talking to *him*, of all people, about fish dreams. Up until a little over a month ago, he'd been celibate for the last few years. And now that he was putting his skills back to use, he always practiced safe sex.

"Why does Kaleb always have to be late?" Kael grumbled as he walked over to look out the window. "I'm hungry as hell."

"Cool your heels, Kael Strong. You think I don't know you been sneaking in the kitchen, picking at the food?" Lisha shot back at him calmly.

Their children all laughed as Kael suddenly belched and then looked contrite.

"Hungry my ass," Lisha grumbled.

Kahron dropped down onto the sofa, beside Kade. "There's talk you and Garcelle were looking mighty cozy riding a horse together last week," he said for Kade's ears only.

Kade shrugged. "Small-town talk. Small-town assumptions. Welcome to Holtsville, little brother."

"Funny thing about small-town talk and small-town assumptions . . . Sometimes they're right on point," Kahron drawled as he took Kade's beer from his hand to take a sip. "Whether we want them to be or not."

"Hey, Ma," Kade called out, just as calm as could be. "I bet Kahron and Bianca are the reason for those fish dreams."

Kade ignored his brother's swear and the evil eye Bianca shot him as he picked up the remote to flip through the channels.

"You two have something you want to say?" Lisha asked as her eyes darted back and forth between Kahron and Bianca.

"No!" they shouted out emphatically in unison.

Kade bit back a smile.

The front door swung open, and Kaleb strolled in. "What's the deal, family?"

Kael jumped to his feet and rubbed his hands together. "Dinner's the deal," he said over his shoulder as he made his way into the dining room.

Lisha shook her head as she rose to follow him. "Lord, that man."

Kade and Kahron were the last to follow the family out of the living room. "You and Garcelle disappearing in the woods for hours at a time?" said Kahron. "You best mind those fish dreams ain't all about you, big brother."

"Curiosity killed a nosy-ass cat," Kade drawled as he took his seat at the table, in between Kaeden and Kadina.

Kahron just laughed as he took the seat across the table, next to his wife.

Lisha walked out of the kitchen, carrying a huge platter. She sat it in the middle of the table, amid side dishes of macaroni and cheese, okra stew, white rice, and corn bread. She cleared her throat as she took her seat.

"Lisha Mae Strong, now enough is enough!" Kael roared as he looked down at the big platter of fried fish. "I thought you said you were frying chicken."

Lisha cocked her eyebrow as she eyed each and every one of her children.

Kade shook his head before he reached over to kiss the top of Kadina's head.

Bianca and Kahron looked at each other before they paid way too much attention to fixing their plates.

Kaitlyn reached in her purse and slapped her birth control pills on the table as she calmly poured a glass of lemonade.

"I wish somebody would go ahead and piss on the damn stick," Kaleb grumbled before he focused on piling his plate high with food.

Kaeden reached in his pocket for his inhaler.

"Daddy, what's with all the talk about fish lately?" Kadina whispered to him.

Kade scooped rice onto her plate and then topped

it with a spoonful of okra stew. "We'll talk about it later," he whispered, praying like hell they didn't attract his mother's attention. The woman was on an all-out mission.

"Papa Kael, thanks so much for making the okra stew," said Bianca. "I have been—"

"*Craving*?" Lisha asked delicately as she glanced at Bianca before taking a bite of her food. "I remember each time I was pregnant, I would crave cheesecake. Had it so bad each and every time that Kael would start buying Pampers as soon as I started asking for cheesecake."

Bianca just massaged her temples with her fingers.

"*Anyway*, we brought you all here because we have good news," Kael said, ignoring his wife as he rose to his feet. "In December your mother and I are going on a two-week cruise to Negro, Jamaica—"

"*Negril*, Jamaica," Lisha corrected him around a bite of food.

"Yeah, right," said Kael as he rubbed his hands together. "It's time I really start enjoying my retirement full time. So, Kade, I'll be relying on you more than ever, Son."

"No worries, Pops," Kade said. "It's well deserved . . . for both of you."

A round of questions about anything and everything concerning their trip followed, and then Kade watched as Kahron rose to his feet, with his glass raised. "Here's to working hard and learning how to play even harder. It is time to sit back and enjoy the fruits of your labor—"

"*And* the fruits of my children's loins," Lisha added.

Kael dropped his head in his hand as everyone at the table dropped their forks and released a long, heavy breath.

* * *

Garcelle glanced at her watch as she sat in her car in the parking lot of the movie theater. Kade was running late for their date. "Humph, date," she said, only slightly sarcastic. "For a real date, the man picks the woman up at her house, and they ride together to the movies. They don't meet in separate cars, like two bad-ass adulterers."

She watched the couples arriving and walking into the movie theater together. It irked the hell out of her. *I must be PMSing*, she thought as she picked up her ringing cell phone.

"Hey, you."

"Kade, I've been calling you for twenty minutes," she said, sitting up in the seat of her car.

"I must have turned the volume down on my phone."

"Where are you?" she asked as she scratched an itch in the palm of her hand.

Knock-knock.

She nearly jumped out of her skin as Kade bent down to look through the driver's side window of her car. She slapped the phone closed as he opened the door for her. "Come on. The movie's started."

Kade frowned. "Are you mad?" he asked, obviously confused.

Garcelle forced a smile as she looked up at him. "No . . . no. Of course not. I just wanted to see the movie. Can we . . . go see the movie?"

Kade's frown deepened.

Garcelle turned and walked up to the line of people, which ran down the stairs of the movie theater. She looked up at Kade briefly as he came up to stand beside her. She had to admit he looked nice in khakis and an orange Hilfiger polo.

"My parents are going on a cruise," he said into the quiet between them.

"That's nice," she said shortly. From the corner of her eye, she saw him wipe his mouth.

"Garcelle, what's going on with you?" he asked, lowering his head to speak directly into her ear.

She gave him another one of those fake smiles that made her face muscles tense. "I wish you'd stop asking me that," she said in a low voice as the line moved forward.

"I wish you'd tell me what's going on with you."

Garcelle stepped aside as they reached the outdoor box-office window. She watched Kade as he paid for their movie tickets. As he walked up beside her and held the door, she avoided his eyes. She was angry, and holding it in, pretending she wasn't angry, was making her even angrier.

"You all right? You want something?" he asked, looking down at her as they passed the snack counter.

"I'm fine."

She felt him tense beside her.

When they walked into the dark theater, the movie was playing, and a loud action sequence of gunfire and bombs coming through the surround sound made it seem like they were in the middle of World War III.

Garcelle followed Kade to a spot near the far wall. She tugged his hand once they settled into the seats. "Are you sure you want us to sit together? Somebody might see us."

"And?" he snapped as he turned in the seat to look at her.

"Hell, it's your issue, not mine," she snapped back.

"*Sshhh.*"

They both ignored that from the people behind them.

"Listen, what the hell is your problem?" said Kade.

"My problem?" she asked, sitting up in the theater seat to face him. "What is *my* problem?"

Kade threw his hands up as if exasperated.

Garcelle crossed her legs and then crossed her arms over her chest as she rocked back and forth in the reclining theater seat, mumbling under her breath in Spanish.

Kade mumbled something unintelligible under his breath.

"What did you say?" Garcelle asked, knowing she was being childish and not caring one bit.

Kade stood up. "I said you're crazy," he said, looking down at her.

"Hey, sit down!" someone yelled from behind them.

Garcelle jumped to her feet. "And you're selfish."

"Y'all need to take that outside," someone else yelled.

"Shut up!" both Garcelle and Kade roared at the theatergoers.

Garcelle pushed past him and stormed out of the theater just as an usher entered. She heard Kade say, "Oh, trust me, we're out of here."

She was walking out of the building and toward her car when she felt a hand wrap around her upper arm. She felt a tingling sensation, and she knew without looking that it was Kade. She pulled away from him. "Just leave me alone, Kade," she said coldly as she reached in her purse for her keys.

"You want me to leave you alone?" he asked just

as coldly, moving up to walk beside her. "You ain't said nothing but a word."

He quickly walked past her, climbed into his SUV, and sped away, without giving her a second look.

Garcelle fought the urge to flip him off, jumped in her car, and sped away as well.

Kade slammed his hand on the wheel in frustration. He was still lost as to what the hell had just happened. The Garcelle who acted like a child needing to be spanked was not the fiery, up-front woman he thought he was involved with. This night was nothing but drama with a capital *D*, and it wasn't something he had the time or patience for. Ever. Period.

He pulled up to a red light and glanced down at his cell phone, which was sitting on the passenger seat. He patted his hand on his thigh in time to the music playing on the stereo as his eyes kept darting to his phone. He shook his head. "I'm not calling her," he told himself aloud as he pulled away.

What he had thought was going to be a fun night out with his woman had turned into one of the most embarrassing and frustrating spectacles of his life. Catch a flick. Maybe go by Ye Old-Fashioned Café for ice cream and then spend the night at their favorite hotel. How the hell had those plans become a hollering match in the middle of a movie theater?

Kade had just left Charleston and entered Summerville when he picked up his phone and turned it off. He wasn't sure if Garcelle even wanted to call and talk to him, but he did know that they both needed a little time to cool off.

* * *

Garcelle couldn't sleep. She would doze for an hour and then jump up and check her cell phone to see if Kade had called. She truly needed her sleep. She had her first pathophysiology test in the morning. She tossed. She turned. She knew she would have bags as big as one of her textbooks under her eyes.

She sat up in bed and picked up her cell phone, which lay by her pillows. This couldn't be the end for Kade and her. Could it? Not over a silly little argument in a movie theater. It was not like anyone there had known them, right? They hadn't said anything yet that they couldn't get past, right?

They needed to talk.

She dialed Kade's cell phone number, but then she stopped, her thumb hovering over the SEND button.

It was one in the morning. Maybe he was sleeping. She couldn't believe she felt nervous about calling her man. She was being ridiculous. She hit SEND.

"Your call is being transferred to an automated voice mail system."

She sat up straight in the bed. His phone was turned off. "Oh no, he didn't," she muttered to herself as she dialed him again.

"Your call is being transferred to an automated voice mail system."

Garcelle fought the urge to leave him a voice mail before she turned off her phone and flopped back down on the bed in frustration.

The next morning, before the sun even began to rise, Kade busied himself getting Kadina ready for school. His daughter wasn't exactly a morning riser, and she grumbled as he led her into the bathroom. "Teeth. Face. Wash. Underwear change. Go," he told her, placing fresh undergarments on the sink before he left the bathroom. He walked in her bedroom to find out which of her new outfits she'd chosen to wear.

Not that he had anything to worry about. Garcelle had taken her shopping, and each coordinated outfit had been hung in her closet, with a little Polaroid pinned to each one showing which shoes to wear with it. Garcelle had really tried to make sure that everything ran smoothly during Kadina's first couple of weeks of school.

He smiled at her thoughtfulness.

Kadina dragged herself into her bedroom. "Why can't it still be summer, Daddy?" she asked as she came to stand in front of where he sat on the edge of her bed.

He chuckled as he held the jeans for her to step into. "Because your job is to go to school and get good grades, so your vacation is over, kiddo," he told her as he zipped up her pants and buckled her sparkly belt.

"One day I'm going to work on the ranch with you, just like Aunt Bianca works with her daddy," she told him as she raised her arms over her head for him to put on her pink- and white-striped polo shirt.

"Oh, you are?"

Kadina nodded. "I'm never leaving *my* daddy," she said, with the utmost confidence of a child.

Kade snorted as he handed her her matching pink sweater jacket. "We'll revisit this when you're thirteen," he said dryly.

She jumped on the end of the bed, beside him, and threw her legs onto his lap so that he could pull on her socks and sneakers. "Daddy, can I try to tie them again?" she asked.

He nodded and watched as she knelt on the floor and fought like hell to tie the laces herself. Another Garcelle contribution. Kadina wasn't quite there, and Kade had to tighten the loops, but she was on the road to her first bit of independence.

She grabbed her bucket of hair accessories before she knelt between his legs, with her arms over his thighs. "One pom-pom, please," she said. "And do it like Garcelle."

Kade frowned as he loosened the band in her hair and rubbed her hair with hair grease before he brushed her edges back up. "I'll do it the best I can," he said, his face determined as he twisted the band back around her hair.

She handed him three pink and white balls to wrap round the curly Afro puff atop her head.

He thought about Garcelle. About leaving for work in the morning without his belly filled with her strong and sweet coffee and homemade breakfast pastries. About the scent of her perfume no longer lingering round the house. About not coming home to her in the night. About their argument last night. About not speaking to her all night.

"Yeah, I miss her, too," he admitted as he felt a literal pang in his heart.

Kadina jumped up and checked her appearance in her mirror. She nodded in satisfaction before she turned back to press her forehead against Kade's. "You're a good daddy," she whispered to him before puckering her lips.

"Now that's the best compliment I've ever received." He kissed her briefly before rising to his feet. "Let's go have some waffles before the school bus comes."

"With strawberry syrup?" she asked as she left the room.

"What else is there?" he joked, grabbing her rolling book bag as he left her room.

Kade was sitting in front of Garcelle's house when she walked out the front door. She paused on the top step of the porch as her eyes locked with his through his windshield. He was glad to see her, even though a big piece of him was still annoyed at the way she'd acted last night.

Garcelle looked away as she closed and locked the front door before she jogged down the stairs. She specifically ignored him as she climbed into her car.

Here he'd thought, after a night of both of them cooling their heels, she would be ready to have an adult conversation. *Hell with it.* He was starting to wonder if jumping into a relationship with Garcelle had been the right choice.

"Kade."

He turned his head. His eyes filled with surprise when he saw Garcelle standing beside his driver's side window. He lowered the window farther. "Are we going to argue like we did in the movie theater?" he asked.

Garcelle stepped forward. "Listen, I should have come out and said what was bothering me last night . . . what has been bothering me for the last few weeks. You *did* ask—"

"Several times," he insisted, with a hard look.

"Kade. I mean seriously. *Seriously.*" Garcelle tilted

her head back and shook it before she looked at him again.

If she acts up again, I'm pulling away and leaving her here to argue by her damn self, he thought. "Garcelle—"

"Let me finish apologizing before you give me one of your speeches."

He swallowed his irritation. "What do you mean one of my speeches?" he balked.

Garcelle snorted in derision. "Kade, please, you can get on your little soapbox when you want . . . but can we stay in the moment please?"

Kade smirked. "If you could define what the moment is exactly, maybe I'd be more successful at staying in it."

"You are a smart ass," she snapped.

"And you have a bad attitude."

"You're selfish."

"And the way you acted last night was childish."

"Oh, and turning off your phone wasn't."

"No more than you turning off yours, too."

"Why do you love tit for tat?"

"Why do you think you can say whatever and do whatever whenever you get ready?"

Garcelle sat her hands on her hips as she looked down at her sneakers and sighed heavily. "Kade . . ."

"Yeah," he said briefly.

"I don't like feeling like we're sneaking around like two kids whose parents don't want them to date or like two married people having an affair."

Kade reached to shut his vehicle off. "Garcelle—"

"No, let me finish," she said as she shook her head, making her ponytail do a dance. "I mean, maybe for you it feels like an affair, since you live as if you're still married, but I'm just curious, Kade Strong—"

"Oh, I'm back to Kade Strong," he drawled as he tilted his head back against the headrest and wiped his eyes with his hands.

"I'm not joking, Kade."

"Garcelle, trust me. I know I'm not married," he said, unable to deny the tinge of bitterness in his voice.

"Reema is—"

Kade's face hardened. "Don't go there, Gar—"

Her eyes dulled, and her lips thinned to a line.

Kade couldn't believe they were in the midst of their second argument. *Reema would never act like this. . . .*

"What?" Garcelle asked, stepping closer to him after witnessing the sudden change of expression on his face.

Kade released a heavy breath as he looked at her. The comparison to Reema was completely out of line, and he just *thanked* God he'd thought it and hadn't said it. The taste of that foot would've been bitter.

Garcelle wanted the next step in their relationship. She wanted more from him. What seemed so simple for her was so very complicated for him, but then was it fair for her?

"Okay. Listen, Garcelle. Let's take a shortcut," he said as he opened the car door and turned sideways in his seat to face her.

She looked a little alarmed but, thankfully, said nothing as she crossed her arms over her chest.

"One of the things I like about you is how open and honest you are. You say what you feel. You don't hide anything." He leaned forward and reached for her arms to pull her forward. She moved to him with obvious reluctance. The scent of her flowery perfume teased him. "Last night was frustrating as hell for me. So I ask that next time you have something on your mind, just come out and tell me. Don't leave me to guess, and then when I still don't get it, you get more shitty than ever."

Garcelle squinted like she was 'bout to cuss him twelve ways to Sunday.

Kade went on. "Now, I admit that I wanted to keep people out of our business, but now I agree we're two grown-ass people who shouldn't be sneaking around town and out of town to see each other. I promise to do better if you promise not to act up in public again."

Garcelle placed her hands on his knees. "Good shortcut," she said, with a hint of a smile.

Kade leaned forward to press his lips to hers.

"I'm sorry," she whispered against his mouth.

He leaned his forehead against hers. "So am I."

"So no more down low?" she asked.

Kade knew his options were simple. To have Garcelle meant a full-blown relationship. Telling Kadina—who had already dropped enough hints for him to know this was right up her alley. Family functions. Public displays of affection. Nosy country people keeping an eye on them and everything they did. He knew their relationship would be the talk of Holtsville. There was no turning back.

He didn't want to lose her. He wasn't going to lose her. Not over this.

"I refuse to even use the words *down low* . . . but, yes," he finally said, with a laugh.

Garcelle stepped closer to him and wrapped her arms around his waist. She smiled, and in his heart, he felt emotions he wasn't quite ready to claim.

It scared and excited him all at once.

16

Garcelle felt like she was under a microscope as she shopped at the small store near the mobile home park. She glanced over her shoulder, and a few of the women in the store were openly staring at her. She stared back at them before she turned back around to place her items on the counter. The clerk, Keisha, gave Gabrielle a stare filled with attitude as she scratched her orange short-cropped weave.

She kept giving Garcelle the once over as she took her slow and sweet time ringing up the items. "Six–fifty," Keisha said, with a surly tone.

"Humph. She a slick little something, too. Word all over Holtsville how she wouldn't let a woman within five feet of him, and now *she* dating him. Oh, that heifer slick."

"Good and slick."

Garcelle turned again to find Rita and Pita looking as scandalous as ever in skirts that were hardly as long as men's underwear. "Do you ladies have something you want to say *about* me *to* me?" Garcelle asked, with a big, fake grin.

Keisha rudely dropped Garcelle's change on the wooden counter. One of the quarters spun on its side before it rolled off the counter and onto the floor. "Oops, my bad," she said, with not a hint of regret in her voice.

"No problem. Mistakes happen," said Garcelle. She laughed a little as she bent over and picked up the coin. "You know what's funny?" She eyed each of the three women, even though none of them answered her question.

"Well, I'll tell you what's funny. You all act like I blocked each of *you* from getting him." She moved her index finger in between the sisters. "You two got like a dozen kids between the two of you. And, Keisha, most men who know you say you'll screw a snake. *So* . . . none of y'all had a chance in hell with him. So I didn't block a damn thing, sweethearts. And sitting around, thinking *I'm* the reason you couldn't get Kade Strong, now *that's* funny as hell." Garcelle chuckled as she walked out the door just as calm as could be.

Garcelle liked how she and Kade blurred the line between friendship and love: they could get lost in the heat of lovemaking or just hang out, laughing and talking as cool-ass friends.

She was turning down the road leading into the mobile home park when her new cell phone vibrated on the passenger seat.

"Hey, you," she said, already knowing it was Kade. "What's up?"

"I was just thinking about you," she admitted, with a soft smile. "I miss you, lover."

"Tell me in Spanish."

Garcelle pulled her car into the front yard of the trailer. "*Te echo de menos, amor,*" she said in her huskiest voice.

"And last night on the phone, what did you say you wanted to do to me?"

Garcelle rolled down the windows as the car got hotter. "*Te quiero lamer de los pies a la cabeza,*" she whispered to him, making her Spanish accent more prominent, because she knew it turned him on even more.

"Everywhere?" he asked thickly.

"*Sí,*" she said, with an arch of her eyebrow and a tiny bite of her bottom lip.

Kade cleared his throat. "I'm on my way to pick you up."

Garcelle's heart raced at the thought of seeing him. "Should I bring the naughty maid costume or the bunny?" she asked as she climbed out of her car.

"Either one is fine as long as you wear a nice dress for church over it."

Garcelle froze. "Church? You want me to go to church with you . . . *this* morning?" she asked.

"That's right."

Garcelle smiled. This would be their first public appearance. This would really get the gossipmongers on the grind. "I'll be ready when you get here," she said, her heart swelling with emotion for him.

"We," he said. "When *we* get there."

"We?" she asked.

"Kadina and I are on the way."

"That's perfect," she said before she walked into the house.

* * *

Kael was jolted from sleep when his wife nudged him. He looked around to see if anyone else had caught him sleeping in church.

"What do you think *that* means, Kael?" whispered Lisha.

He followed his wife's line of vision and saw Kade, Garcelle, and Kadina walking into church together. "Well, well, well," he said low in his throat. He gave his son a thumbs-up as they took their seats in a crowded pew in the rear of the church.

"Kael," Lisha whispered to him sharply as she pulled his hand back down to his waist.

"You the one taking my attention off the minister to be nosey."

Lisha glared at him as she leaned over closer to him. "Well, the minister must have been in your dreams, 'cause in anther minute you would've been calling in the hogs," she whispered.

"Ssshhh."

They both looked indignant at Sister Ollie, who had turned around in her seat and was giving them the evil eye as the rose on the edge of her hat flip-flopped from right to left. The woman was one of the biggest gossips in Holtsville. She could spread a rumor quicker than the clap ran through a whorehouse.

"She needs to focus on the sermon and stop eaves-dropping for some news to carry," said Kael. He made an odd face at her, and he swore that rose was going to fly right off as she whipped back around in her seat.

Out of the corner of her eye, Portia Klinton looked at Kade as she snuggled closer to him in the pew and then slowly crossed her legs, before hitching the hem of her skirt up higher on her thigh.

When that didn't catch his eye, she dropped her hymnbook and then bent over in her seat to pick it up, giving him a healthy view of the shape of her derriere. When he ignored that, she leaned over to him, with her breast pressed against his arm, and whispered, "You really should call me. . . ."

Kade leaned back and drawled, "You're here to pick up the Word and not men, *Sister* Portia."

Portia was more than surprised when he rose up a little in his seat and switched places with his daughter. "Oh no, he didn't," she mouthed as he reached for Garcelle's hand and held it atop his thigh.

"Are you okay, Sister Portia? You don't look so good," whispered Kadina.

Portia scowled as she looked down into Kadina's perky face. She uncrossed her legs, pushed her skirt back down to her knees, and faced forward to focus on the minister.

Kadina could hardly believe the sight of her father and Garcelle holding hands. Her daddy had said they were dating—which meant boyfriend and girlfriend in her world. She loved it!

She splayed her hands and began ticking off her fingers. They could go to the movies together. And out to eat together. And Garcelle could teach her more Spanish. And they could all go to church together every Sunday. And she would probably have little brothers and sisters one day.

Oh boy, she thought as she let her feet swing back and forth in the pew and looked at her hands again. *I love it!*

* * *

Kaeden tried to pretend that he was not watching Jade's striking profile from where he sat in the pew behind her in church. He tried and failed miserably. The woman made his palms sweat.

When she happened to glance over her shoulder in his direction, Kaeden hurriedly look over his shoulder so that she didn't catch him staring at her like a perv. His eyes happened to lock with those of his niece, Kadina. He smiled as she motioned at her father and Garcelle before she gave him the okay signal with her hand.

He was turning back around in his seat when Sister Portia sent him a subtle wink. His mind wasn't on her and her foolishness.

Garcelle and Kade. First, Kahron and Bianca. Now Kade's dating Garcelle. What next? Kaleb settling down? Good grief. He was the responsible brother. He was the rational and reasonable one. The one most suited to family life. His brothers had run through more women than he could count. Not that he was a monk.

He stole a quick look at Jade. Suddenly, naughty thoughts of Jade's voluptuous frame flashed in his head. He cleared his throat and ran his finger around a collar that was suddenly way too tight. *Those* thoughts certainly weren't appropriate for church.

All he could do was ask the Lord to forgive him as he fought like hell to keep his eyes off of Jade Prince.

Kahron's stomach grumbled where he sat between Kaleb and Bianca in church. His wife nudged him, with a wrinkle in her brow, as she eyed him. Kaleb chuckled beside him.

He was starving, and he couldn't help it if his

stomach was reading him the riot act. He noticed his parents turn in their seats, and curiosity made him follow their line of vision. His mouth dropped open.

Small-town talk. Small-town gossip, my ass. Kahron winced. *Uh, forgive me Lord.*

He nudged Bianca and Kaleb, motioning for them to check out Garcelle and Kade. They looked over their shoulders as well.

Kaleb grunted in laughter as he turned back around in his seat. "Looks like the maid hunt is back on, bro. Another one has bit the dust."

Kahron was happy for his brother, *but* Garcelle was his *sixteenth* housekeeper since he'd moved into his own home. Sixteen in less than five years. Was he cursed? Kahron frowned deeply.

"Aww," Bianca cooed to him softly as she took his hand in hers, with a soft laugh.

Kade swallowed hard and looked away when he discovered Carlos Santos's set of coal black eyes staring at him. He crossed his ankle over his knee as he settled back into his seat on the living-room couch. His face warmed when he thought of the first night he ever made love to Garcelle . . . right on that very living-room floor. He cleared his throat.

"So how long have you and my Garcelle been dating?" Carlos asked, his accent pronounced as he leaned forward in his recliner to offer Kade a cigar.

"Close to two months."

"And this is the first that I know about you two." Carlos nodded as he frowned. "Interesting."

"Do you disapprove?" Kade asked, unfolding his leg to lean forward and rest his elbows on his knees.

"Of the relationship . . . no. Of your secrecy . . . yes."

Kade nodded. He felt like a teenage boy being grilled by his girlfriend's father. He thought of his own love for and protection of Kadina, and had nothing but patience for this man, whom he respected.

"So is that where she has been staying out all night?" Carlos asked, with a critical eye at Kade.

"Daddy!" Garcelle gasped as she walked into the living room, having changed out of the dress she'd worn to church earlier. "We are not children who need to be supervised."

Kade was relieved to see her. He honestly didn't know what Carlos was going to ask him next.

Carlos tilted back in his recliner as he lit his cigar. "When Juan wanted to date my Marisol, he came to me first for my permission before they even went on a date. When he wanted to marry her, he came to me first and asked for my permission before he even proposed. There is a way to do things. That is *all* I'm saying."

"Papi—"

"No, Garcelle. Your father is talking to me, so I'll address him," Kade said, looking Carlos directly in the eyes. "I must be honest that it didn't cross my mind to ask your permission to date Garcelle. In truth, it's not something I or anyone I know has ever done. I'm not judging it. I'm just being honest. You see a pretty woman, you want to get to know her better, and you ask *her* if she wants to spend time with you to get to know you better as well. You date and you see if something serious can or will develop, and *then* you bring in the whole meeting of the families."

Carlos nodded as he continued to smoke his cigar. He looked at Kade through the smoke.

"So my way is different from your way. It's just a simple misunderstanding, and no disrespect was meant at all," said Kade. He looked up at Garcelle and then back at Carlos. "We've known each other for years. I know you're a good man, just like you know I'm a good man."

Carlos looked at Kade a long time—man to man. "And your heart is free to love another?" Carlos asked.

The question threw Kade off.

"Papi, we just started dating," Garcelle said, her words filling the silence. She walked over to Kade and held out her hand to him. "Come on. Let's go outside."

Kade rose to his feet. He stepped closer to where Carlos sat and held out his hand to him.

Carlos stuck his cigar between his teeth before he begrudgingly accepted Kade's hand.

Kade followed Garcelle out the door and to the front yard. "Talk about putting a man's feet to the fire," he joked lightly as they sat down on the front steps.

"I'm just glad my two crazy uncles weren't home." Kade just smiled.

Kadina came running into the yard, with Paco hot on her heels. She ran to the bottom step of the porch. "Home base," she screamed as she panted heavily.

Paco stopped short as he swiped his long bangs out of his eyes. "Okay, this time you're it," he said before he knelt down into a runner's stance and then took off.

"Bye, Daddy. Bye, Garcelle," Kadina hollered over

her shoulder before she flew off the porch and raced behind Paco, toward the rear of the trailer park.

Garcelle laughed at them. "I'm glad you and Kadina came to visit me here at my home," she told Kade as he massaged her neck beneath the soft layers of her hair.

"Me, too," he told her, fighting the urge to kiss her nape as she bent over, her head near her open thighs, with a soft moan.

"I miss you when we're not together," he admitted freely.

"Me, too, lover."

He used both his hands to massage her shoulders.

"That *feels* so good, Kade."

Just knowing he was making her feel good was making him feel hot. He felt himself harden between his thighs. Would thing ever cool off between them? "It'll be getting cool soon," he said, seeking a diversion from his erotic thoughts as he continued to knead her shoulders.

"Hmmm."

"I was thinking next Saturday we could take the kids to the pond and have that picnic," he offered.

Garcelle looked over her shoulder at him. "I would love that, especially including Paco. We're very close. Much closer than either of us is to our older sister."

Kade shifted on the step and lifted his leg over Garcelle so that she was sitting between his thighs. "You hardly talk about her."

"I hardly know her. She moved to Texas when I was in high school. She's a lot older than me. We talk on the phone some, but she has her life, and we have ours."

Kade frowned at the obvious distance between

them, but he said nothing. He focused on putting his hands to work.

"You know, I had no idea you were such a good masseur," Garcelle said from beneath the layers of her hair. "I can only imagine what you could do if I was stretched out on a bed."

Kade's hands paused at the image of Garcelle, nude and gleaming with oil, as she lay on her stomach as he massaged her calves, the backs of her thighs, her buttocks, and her lower back. He would start with his hands but then would use his lips to taste every delicious inch of the soft skin covering the toned muscles of her body. Garcelle had the kind of body that made a Coca-Cola bottle look as straight as a ruler.

Garcelle looked over her shoulder at him again. Their eyes locked, and his heart raced when he saw her eyes were smoldering.

The interior of the SUV was hot and dark as Garcelle lowered the front passenger seat and climbed into the backseat, where Kade sat waiting for her. Being in the backseat of his SUV, surrounded by trees and dense brush on a dark and lonely country road, made everything about this heated moment so intense. *Very* intense. They giggled. They kissed. They whispered to each other. They bumped into each other as they struggled to remove their clothes.

Down to her panties and bra, Garcelle straddled his hips. There was just enough of the moon's light to see his handsome face as she unsnapped her lace bra to free her breasts. Instantly, he brought his hands up to massage them. At the feel of his hands and his mouth on her nipples, she gasped hotly and arched her back.

"Kade," she moaned as she reached down between them to stroke his curved hardness.

Kade pressed the condom into her hands and clenched his jaw as she quickly covered his length. He slid his fingers inside Garcelle's panties and roughly pushed them to the side. He lifted her slightly, with an arm around her waist, then lowered her.

"What if someone catches us?" she whispered against his chin before she bit it lightly.

"Everyone knows if the SUV is rocking, you don't come knocking." Kade planted rushed and heated kisses over her face as he moved his hands down to grab the softness of her buttocks. They both gasped as her warm and wet tightness surrounded him like a sleeve.

They laughed a little before Garcelle began to work her hips. The steam their bodies created rose to coat and fog the windows of the SUV as it rocked gently from left to right.

17

Bianca looked up as Mimi and her father walked into her kitchen, hand in hand. Kahron followed behind them and leaned in the doorway. Bianca's face filled with surprise. "I didn't know you were in town, Mimi," she said, rising to her feet to hug her close.

"I just got in a few minutes ago, sweetie, and we came straight over here."

The new Mimi—or was it the old Beulah—took a little getting used to. *Thank God she's found a happy medium,* Bianca thought as she reclaimed her seat. She had compromised: she was midway between the over-the-top Mimi and the dowdy Beulah. Her hair was in a classic bob, and she wore minimal make-up on her still-beautiful and refined features, but gone were the 1980s *Dynasty* suits, the bulky jewelry, and the Beverly Hills cowgirl garb, replaced by a simple fitted silk T and linen slacks, with crocodile flats. Mostly, that voice was gone. Her sharp sense of humor had remained, and for that, Bianca was grateful.

"Are you in for the weekend?" asked Bianca as she leaned back against Kahron, who stood behind her.

"No, she'll be staying for a while," Hank said vaguely, with a hearty smile, as he sat down on one of the stools.

They looked at each other.

Bianca's eyes darted from one to the other. "What?" she asked, sensing there was more. She turned slightly to look up at Kahron, but he just shrugged.

Mimi pulled her hand from the pocket of her pants and extended her arm to them. A good-sized solitaire twinkled from her left ring finger.

"Is that an engagement ring?" Bianca asked as she escaped from Kahron's hold and grabbed Mimi's smooth hand with both of hers. Her mouth dropped open as Mimi smiled.

"Congratulations, old man," Kahron said, stepping around the island to shake Hank's beefy hand.

"Thank you, Son. Thank you," said Hank.

"Ms. Mimi, welcome to the family," said Kahron. He literally picked her up off her feet and twirled her before he planted a kiss on her cheek.

"Oh, come on, Kahron. You have Bianca, and I have Hank. There could never be anything between us," Mimi joked as she playfully fluttered her lashes at him.

Everyone laughed. Everyone but Bianca. She gave them all a hesitant smile as three sets of eyes turned on her. She met each look.

Her father sought approval. Mimi sought acceptance. Kahron wanted peace.

Mimi and her father were getting married. It took a minute to get used to the idea. The minute was over. She had never seen her father happier, and who was she to block him?

Her father jumped to his feet, with a stern look. "Bianca—"

"Kahron, baby, will you get a bottle of sparkling cider for us? Looks like we have some celebrating to do," Bianca said, pulling Mimi to her for a tight embrace before she moved over to hug her father.

"That's my girl," Hank said as he gave her a big bear hug.

Kahron handed each of them a flute. "Here's to a life filled with lots of love and happiness for you both."

"Hear! Hear!" they all said in unison.

Bianca placed a hand on her flat stomach as she smiled into her flute. "Since we're celebrating, anyway, now is a good time. I've been trying to figure out a really cute way to tell you something, Kahron."

Kahron's eyes darted to her, over the rim of his flute.

Bianca sat her flute on the island, then picked up her purse and dug into it. "Your mama and her damn fish dreams," she said softly, holding up the pregnancy stick as she looked into her husband's loving eyes.

Hank jumped to his feet. "Hot diggity damn!"

Kahron almost dropped his flute to the floor as he crossed the kitchen and pulled Bianca close against him. He picked her up and sat her on the counter and stood between her legs. "I love you so much, Bianca Strong," he whispered before he captured her lips with his own.

She was touched by the brightness of his eyes, hinting at tears she knew he wouldn't let fall. She caressed his silvery stubble with her hand as she smiled into his eyes. Eyes that she hoped their child inherited. They were having a baby, and she'd never loved him more.

That Sunday afternoon after church, Kade paused as he entered the kitchen, and all conversation came to an immediate halt at the sight of him. Five pairs of female eyes locked on him. His mother's, his sister's, his sister-in-law's, his daughter's, and his girlfriend's.

"Hello, ladies," he said, throwing them a charming smile.

"Hello," they all said in unison, with soft smiles.

"I, uh, just wanted to grab some beers for me and the fellas."

Garcelle cast him a soft smile before she walked over to the refrigerator. "How many would you like?"

He moved into the kitchen and walked past the ladies to reach Garcelle. He looked down into her laughing eyes. "Were you all talking about me?" he asked her as his eyes dipped down to her lips.

She nodded as she began to pass him the beers one by one.

"Good things?" he asked.

"Great things," she told him as she reached up to press her fingers to his lips.

He kissed them softly as he looked down into her eyes. His heart exploded in his chest, and he didn't think he could stop the words if he tried. "I love you, Garcelle," he whispered to her fiercely. "I really love you."

Her eyes widened and then softened before they smoldered. "Good. Because I love you, too."

"Get a room, you two," Kaitlyn called from across the kitchen, sending Kadina into a fit of giggles.

"I better go," he said, bending his head to taste her lips.

All the ladies sighed.

"Tell me again," Garcelle whispered.

Kade moved his mouth near her ear. "I love you," he repeated, with ease.

With one last kiss to the side of her head, Kade turned and strode out of the kitchen, with a wink at his mother.

"Well, whatever he said to you sure has put a big old Kool-Aid grin on your face," Bianca teased as she stirred a big bowl of potato salad.

Garcelle couldn't stop smiling, but she didn't share with them what had just passed between her and Kade. She would remember it always. A woman never forgets the first time her man tells her that he loves her.

"You ladies are discovering something that I have known for nearly forty years," Lisha said as she smiled warmly at Bianca and Garcelle. "There is nothing—and I do mean nothing—like the love of a Strong man. Take it from the one who has the original. They live up to their names, ladies, they live up to their names."

"*Doh*, Mama," Kaitlyn joked.

"I don't mean just in the bedroom, daughter," Lisha said as she looked at Kaitlyn. "See a real man . . . a real good man . . . is good in *and* out of the bed. He got more going for him than what's below the waist. He got a lot going on in his head and his heart. That's a Strong man, baby, and I love mine."

Bianca grabbed the bottle of wine and topped off

everyone's glass. She gave herself and Kadina more lemonade. "Well, here's to the Strong men."

The women all lifted their glasses.

"Hear! Hear!" they all said in unison.

"*And* to the future generations of Strong men and women," Lisha said warmly, giving Kadina a hug before she winked at Bianca.

"Garcelle . . . Garcelle . . . wake up, baby. We're here."

Garcelle stirred in her sleep and sat up in the seat. She looked out the window of Kade's Expedition. "Where are we?" she asked as she stretched.

"At the hotel," he said as he climbed out of the SUV and came around to open her door.

"The hotel? Why are we at the hotel?" she asked out loud as she slipped her feet into her sandals and grabbed her purse.

She accepted his outstretched hand. "Kade, Kadina stayed in Walterboro with your grandparents. Why didn't we just stay at your house?"

"I thought you would like this better," he told her as they walked into the hotel lobby.

Garcelle stopped in her tracks. He turned. She looked at him appraisingly. His eyes shifted from hers. She tugged on his hand. He looked up and locked his eyes with hers. She raised a brow. Kade smiled. She felt a tugging at her heart.

Love was an amazing thing. She pushed any doubts she had aside and followed him into the hotel lobby.

Kade carried Garcelle into the unlit suite, using his foot to nudge the door closed. She caressed his face, then bent her head to nuzzle his neck as she talked to him softly in Spanish.

He swung her onto the bed, and she stood, towering over him. The sliver of light through the crack in the curtain offered just enough illumination to silhouette the curves of her body as she kicked off one shoe and then the other. She reached up to unzip the lavender sundress she wore.

Kade ran his hands from her ankles to the firm contours of her calves and then to her thighs before massaging her soft buttocks. The dress fell to her waist, and he grabbed the material and jerked it the rest of the way down her body.

"Yes, Kade," she gasped as she reached up to release her hair from its ponytail.

He slid his fingers beneath the lacy rim of her panties to play in her soft curls before he slipped two firm fingers up inside her moistness. She bent her legs to receive them, with a hot gasp, as she rotated her hips against his hand.

"Garcelle," he said thickly before he removed the fingers and then slipped them into his mouth, with a deep groan.

Garcelle kicked her leg high, almost losing her balance, and rested it on his shoulder. He turned his head and pressed his nose and mouth to the soft and warm flesh of her thick thigh as he inhaled deeply of the scent of her intimacy. She laughed softly and freely before she lifted her leg from his shoulder and did a cartwheel across the bed. She eased off her panties and bra before she crawled on her knees toward the middle of the king-sized bed.

Kade nearly tore the buttons from his shirt as he removed it. His hands fumbled as he removed a condom from his wallet and held it with his teeth as he tore off his belt, pants, and boxers. Naked and hard and ready, he covered as much of his throbbing length as he could as his heart pumped wildly. He crawled on his knees to meet her in the middle of the bed. They came together in a heated rush.

Kisses. Touches. Strokes. Caresses. Skin to skin. Body to body. Furious heartbeats. Panting breaths. Racing pulses. Urgency. Need. Want. Electricity. Desire. Fire.

Garcelle put her hands on the hard contours of Kade's chest and pushed him away. He landed on his back, with his erection pointing up to the ceiling, then watched her shadowy figure move from the bed and climb atop the dresser. Her back was pressed to the mirror above the dresser as she brought her legs up.

Kade held his hard and throbbing penis in his hands as he got up from the bed and walked over to where she waited for him. Panting and wet. Her fresh feminine scent heavy in the air. With one thrust he entered her swiftly.

"Ah," they both gasped.

Kade put his hands on her knees and pushed her back until she touched the mirror. He wished for more light so that he could see his hardness surrounded by her lips. See the way her thick bud was swollen with want for him. See the way she made the length of him wet.

He stroked deep inside of her.

Once. Twice. Three times.

Again and again and again until she lost count. Each thrust brought a deep, guttural moan from her.

He bent down, offering her his tongue to suckle, as he shifted his hands to massage her soft breasts and tease her hard nipples until he felt her walls pulsating and pulling him deeper inside of her.

Garcelle sucked his tongue deeply and brought her hands around to grab his buttocks. She enjoyed the way the hard muscles relaxed and then tensed with each delivery of his strokes.

"I'm coming, Garcelle," he moaned into her open mouth as that urgency caused a warm sensation to float over his entire body.

Garcelle let her tears flow as she felt her body free-fall as she came. He tasted her tears as he moved his hips and buttocks until he thought he would break his back. Then his seed shot from him, with a jolt. She clutched his stiff body as he fought to find the strength to continue stroking inside of her.

"I love you . . . I love you . . . God, I love you," he chanted as he fought for control of his body.

"And I love you," she whispered against his sweaty shoulder as they slumped against each other, exhausted and sated.

Long into the night, as Kade slept with his arm and leg over her as they lay on their side, Garcelle could not find enough peace to sleep. Her thoughts were heavy. The truth was a bitter pill to swallow.

In every way imaginable, Kade had given himself to her. They'd spent time together. He'd introduced her as his girlfriend to his family. He'd told her he loved her.

Yet, not once since they'd become involved had she spent the night or enjoyed more than passing affection inside his home. She had fooled herself into thinking it was because of Kadina. But tonight there had been no excuse. There had been no feasible reason for him to pay for a hotel suite when his home sat empty.

Correction. His home was anything but empty. It was filled to the brim with the ghost of his dead wife. And she knew tonight that there was still a piece of Kade that he was sheltering from her.

And *that* hurt like hell.

Kade knew something was wrong. Late into the night he had reached for Garcelle, but she had seemed to draw away from his touch. Then she hopped out of bed and dashed into the bathroom. When he heard the shower running, he jumped out of bed to join her, but the door was locked. When she came out fully dressed and suggested that they leave so that he could go home and rest for work the next day, she wouldn't meet his eyes.

"Garcelle, what's wrong?" he asked.

"Nothing, Kade. Just go and wash so we can go home," she said, with a light tone, which he didn't buy for a second.

He stared at her long and hard. "I don't read minds, Garcelle, and I don't play games," he told her coldly.

"And I don't play with people's heart and make promises I can't keep," she returned in a stiff voice.

Kade sat down on the edge of the bed. "Now you're giving me riddles?"

"Can we just leave?"

Kade laughed sardonically as he snatched up his clothes and started to get dressed. "Since you're in such a rush, I'll wash when I get home."

Garcelle laughed sarcastically. "Yes, hurry and get

back to your precious house, with your precious memories."

Kade paused in zipping up his pants. "Oh, okay. I see what you're getting at that."

"Yes, I'm getting at the fact that you lied and said you were ready to move on. I'm here, living and breathing and loving you, but I'm not about to fight with a ghost, because it's a losing battle." Garcelle turned away from him, and he saw her shoulders shake with her tears.

He started to go to her, but he stopped himself. "I love you, Garcelle—"

"But you love her more," she said in a soft voice as she looked at him.

Kade dropped his eyes from hers, and he felt the pain he knew he'd caused her.

She dropped the cell phone he'd given her and the keys to his house on the dresser as she passed it on her way to the door. "I can't win against a ghost. I wish you and your memories the very best."

Kade strode across the room and grabbed her arm. "Don't go, Garcelle. Don't do this."

She looked up at him, and her eyes were gorgeous even as they were filled with pain. "I'll call my father to come pick me up. Good-bye, Kade."

She pulled her arm away and walked out of the room. The door closed with the utmost finality, and the sound echoed deep in his soul.

18

Two Weeks Later

"Are you okay, Garcelle?"

Garcelle looked up from her textbook to find her professor smiling down at her, with dentures almost bigger than her thin mouth could hold. "Yes . . . I'm fine," she said, slightly stumbling as she sat up straighter in her chair. The eyes of her classmates were upon her.

"Good," her professor said before she walked away.

Garcelle released a heavy breath as she forced herself to focus in class. She had been daydreaming about Kade . . . again.

She missed him and Kadina. She had only seen him in passing during the last couple of weeks. And each time it had been torture to watch him from a distance and wish things could have been different . . . better.

She heard that as soon as the word hit the streets that their relationship was over, women were back on the Kade hunt. Maybe one of those dozens of women would be able to make him move past his wife's death. Obviously, her love wasn't enough.

As soon as class was over, Garcelle grabbed her books and put on her leather coat to fight the slight chill in the October air. She headed straight out of the building and to her car to drive off the campus in Walterboro to her job at the small diner on the main road in Holtsville.

She washed her hands and tied an apron over her long-sleeve fitted T and jeans. The bell rung, signaling new customers had walked through the door.

"Customers at table six," Donnie, the owner and cook, called back to her. "Let's get it moving, Garcelle."

She snatched up an order pad and pen as she mentally prepared herself for her four-hour shift. "I'm on it, Donnie," she said, walking out to the seating area.

"Welcome to . . . ," said Garcelle as she looked into Kade's face. She forced herself to take a deep breath and to keep her composure.

"Hi, Garcelle," said Kade.

She cleared her throat. "Kade," she said shortly.

"Garcelle, I didn't know you were working here."

She didn't even notice the rest of Kade's brothers or his father until Kahron spoke. Not wanting to run into Kade, she had quit her job at Kahron and Bianca's. "I just started last week. Uh, what would you like to order?" she said.

Garcelle didn't release the breath she was holding until she gave Donnie the orders and ran out the back door of the restaurant. "Keep it cool, Garcelle. Calm down," she admonished herself as she paced. "I can do *this*. I *can* do this."

She walked back inside and stood in the kitchen

while she looked over at Kade's table. "I can't do this," she admitted softly.

"Donnie, I need a cheeseburger platter and two specials," Poochie said as she came into the kitchen.

Garcelle grabbed her arm. "Poochie, take table six for me, and I'll take table twelve."

"No problem," Poochie said over her shoulder as she walked back out of the kitchen.

Garcelle ignored Donnie's eyes on her as she walked out of the kitchen and headed for table twelve.

Kade's heart had been pounding wildly in his chest from the moment he looked up and saw Garcelle. As much as he tried to fight it, his eyes kept drifting to her. Drinking in her presence. Filling his memories with snapshots of her.

Kade focused his attention back on his steak and potatoes, but he had no appetite. He dropped his fork onto his full plate. In the last two weeks, he hadn't wanted to do much of anything. He missed Garcelle like crazy.

"You two have got to be kidding me," Kahron said.

Kade shifted his eyes to his brother. "Excuse me?"

"Kahron," Kael said, with a warning in his tone.

"What point are you proving by making yourself into a damn martyr?" Kahron said, obviously ignoring their father's admonition.

Kade's eyes hardened. "What the hell is that supposed to mean?"

"You're miserable without her, and then you're making everyone around you miserable because you'd rather live life looking like a sad hound dog than allow yourself to be happy with another woman," said Kahron.

Kade looked around the table at his family. "Is Kahron speaking for himself or for all of you?" he asked coolly.

Their silence was all too telling.

Kade rose from the table and tossed his napkin onto his plate of untouched food. "I can't give her what she wants or what she needs, so excuse the hell out of me for giving her a chance to go on with her life and not be led on. If doing that makes me the bad guy, then so be it."

He turned and stormed away from the table. He looked up and saw Garcelle standing there, with a pained look on her face. *Damn.* He knew that she'd heard him. He had spoken nothing but the truth, and he saw by the look in her eyes that the truth hurt her.

But Garcelle was a remarkable woman. She didn't go running in the back to cry or rush to him to cuss him out. She waved good-bye to him like he was just another stranger in the street before she tilted her chin up and focused on her customers.

Kade allowed himself another long look at her before he walked out of the restaurant and climbed into his SUV. He missed Garcelle in his life in every way imaginable. He felt like a piece of him was missing, and that made him feel guilty. Loving Garcelle made him feel like he was forgetting Reema.

When he thought of Garcelle, it was so easy to picture her in his life as his wife, the mother of his children, and the stepmother to Kadina. Going to bed with her at night and waking to her every single morning for the rest of his life. Garcelle was a picture-perfect fit for his life . . . completely knocking Reema and all the years they'd shared out of the way.

Those years with Reema were important to him. She was important to him. How in the hell could he just wipe it all away after a few years? Those years were nothing compared to over a decade of being in love with her.

When Garcelle left him that night at that hotel, he had gone downstairs to watch her from a distance. It had made his soul ache to watch her fight not to cry as she stood in the lobby of the hotel. He wanted to go to her and tell her what she wanted to hear—what she needed to hear—but he couldn't. He would have been lying.

Garcelle's father had once asked him if his heart was free to love her. He remembered pausing, because he was unable to answer that question with honesty. Garcelle deserved more than he could give her. She deserved to be more than a woman living in his dead wife's shadow.

Bianca was so sick and tired of being face-first in a commode. She frowned at the taste in her mouth as she flushed the contents of her stomach. Even after she rose to her feet and rinsed her mouth, she stayed in the bathroom. There was solace in there.

She sighed heavily as she dropped the lid and slumped down onto the commode. *Six or seven more months of this?*

There was a knock at the door, and she rolled her eyes heavenward.

"Bianca . . . baby, you have to come out," Kahron said through the door. "Mimi's here to go over the wedding plans."

She had to swallow back a hysterical giggle. She could literally choke herself for opening her big mouth and talking her father and future stepmother out of eloping to Vegas.

No, have the wedding here at my house. I'll help plan it. Sure, we can put together a nice one in six weeks. Sure, I'm sure.

"What in the hell was I thinking?" she muttered aloud.

Kahron knocked again. "Did you say something, baby?"

Between preparing for Thanksgiving dinner at her house, and the wedding at her house just one week later, and putting up with Lisha, who was driving her crazy with baby talk, Bianca was ready to grab Kahron and fly to Vegas . . . forever.

Three Weeks Later

Fate was dealing Garcelle a cruel hand. After seeing Kade and his family in the restaurant where she worked, she kept bumping into Kade. At the Piggly Wiggly when she was grocery shopping. At Bianca's when she dropped her friend and ex-employer off after a day of shopping in Beaufort. At Kahron and Bianca's ranch when she dropped off the fish stew Bianca begged her to make for her. At the menswear store on Main Street in Walterboro when she took her father there to purchase a new suit.

True, Holtsville and Walterboro were small towns, but it was getting to be a bit ridiculous. Over and over and over again, their paths crossed. Each and every time, they would look at each other, wave, and move on in opposite directions to continue living their separate lives.

"Oh God, not again," Garcelle muttered after she looked up and saw Kade and Kadina stroll into Wal-Mart. Her heart hammered as she whipped her buggy around and headed in the other direction.

"Garcelle! Garcelle!" cried Kadina.

She winced at the sound of Kadina's voice. She couldn't dare ignore her, so she plastered a smile on her face and turned just as Kadina came running up to her. Garcelle took a step back after Kadina lunged at her and then wrapped her thin arms around her. "*Hola*, little girl. How are you?" Garcelle asked as she bent to kiss the top of her head.

"I got all good grades in school, and Daddy's gonna buy me whatever I want," she said, looking up at Garcelle with bright cocoa brown eyes.

"Oh, he is?" Garcelle asked lightly.

"Yup." Kadina looked over her shoulder. "Right, Daddy?"

Garcelle bit the clear gloss from her bottom lip as she finally raised her eyes and looked at Kade. He shoved his hands in the pockets of his jeans as he nodded.

"I said I would buy you something, not anything. There's a difference," he told her, with a grin.

"Sure, Daddy," Kadina said in obvious disbelief.

They all fell into a silence made all the more awkward when Kadina looked from Garcelle to Kade with an expected air. Kade and Garcelle looked at each other for what seemed like endless minutes before they both looked away.

"I better be going," Garcelle said.

"Yeah, we don't want to hold you up," Kade said.

"*Adiós*," Garcelle said softly before turning to walk away from them.

She chanced a quick look back, and her heart broke to see Kadina looking over her shoulder as they walked away.

"It really is over," she whispered aloud to herself as she gave the little girl a final wave before she continued on her way.

The holidays were always a tough time for him. The holidays equaled family, and for so long Kade had felt like his small family was incomplete. The holidays were just a poignant reminder of that. On Thanksgiving mornings in the past, he would wake up to an empty bed and the heavy smell of cooking from the kitchen below. He would go downstairs, sip on coffee, and read the paper as Reema made all of his favorite dishes. On this day his kitchen was just a reminder of what he'd lost.

He jumped from the bed and purposely avoided looking at his wedding picture on the wall opposite the bed. Thanksgiving dinner was at Kahron and Bianca's this year, and he was ready for the noise and chaos that usually ensued when his family got together. He jumped into a fresh pair of pajama bottoms before he strode to Kadina's room.

He chuckled at the way she lay across the middle of the bed, with one arm and one foot hanging off and with all the covers nearly on the floor. "Up and at 'em, Kadina," he said, nudging her shoulder.

She scowled in her sleep and scooted back under what covers were left on her bed.

"Come on. We're going to Uncle Kahron's," he told her as he bent over to scoop her up into his arms.

Kadina opened one eye and stretched, with her arms and legs extended. She closed that eye, and her body went slack as she went back to sleep.

"Girl, I don't know what kind of job you going to have, loving the bed so much," he mused as he shook her gently. "Come on and get up, Kadina."

She stretched again before she wrapped her arms around his neck. "Good morning, Daddy," she said in a throaty voice.

He tried not to wince at her morning breath. "Go brush your teeth before you burn out my nose hairs."

Kadina covered her mouth with both her hands and giggled. "You should brush yours before I lose my eyebrows, Daddy," she said, her voice muffled.

He sat her down at his feet and covered his mouth with both of his hands as well. "Let's both brush. Deal?"

She nodded before she went running off to the bathroom.

Kade dropped his hands as he walked back into his bedroom and then into his private bathroom. He did his morning ritual before he strode back into his bedroom. He turned on the television, then looked in his closet for an outfit other than his usual Dickies uniforms.

Choosing his own outfits took getting used to. Reema had laid out what she thought he should wear, down to his socks and shoes. *Life is so much easier in one of my uniforms,* he thought as he selected a pair of jeans, a crisp white shirt, and a tailored suede blazer.

Garcelle used to love to see him in *anything* except one of his uniforms.

He paused in putting on his clothes at the thought

of her. He shook his head as if to clear his thoughts as he finished getting dressed. "Kadina," he called out.

"I'm right here, Daddy."

He nearly jumped out of his skin at her sudden appearance at his side. "You brought your clothes?" he asked as he flopped down on the end of his bed.

"*Sí*, Papi."

He helped her get dressed in her colorful, opaque stockings and the ruffled jean dress she'd chosen. "Ready for some turkey and stuffing?"

"And macaroni and cheese, and greens, and cranberry sauce," she finished in a little singsong fashion as she did a little dance.

"Then let's get our shoes on, and let's ride."

She winked at him before she went skipping out of the room. "You ain't said nothing but a word, Daddy."

He was slipping on his shoes when Kadina reappeared at his door. He looked up at her face and was surprised by her serious expression. "What's wrong?"

"Daddy, I don't want you to be alone anymore," Kadina said suddenly as she walked into the room and smoothed down his lapels.

"First, I'm not alone, because I have you and a whole bunch of family." Kade looked up at her. "Second, I know you love me and you just want me to be happy, but trust me, I'm okay."

"Don't you think Mama loved you?"

Kade's brows furrowed as he frowned at the question. "Yes, your mama loved me very much."

"Then wouldn't she want you to be happy, too, Daddy?"

Kade paused.

His daughter was right. Reema had been a warm

and caring woman. She had put others before herself. She *wouldn't* want him to be alone.

"I miss hanging out with Garcelle, Daddy."

He nodded. He had a wrenching feeling in his
gut. "Me, too, baby girl. Me, too."

Kade fell silent. Life without Garcelle was hell.
Seeing her around town, and having to fight his
urge to go to her, tore him up. He hadn't been
back in Donnie's restaurant since the day he found
out she was working there. It took everything he
had not to go to her.

Garcelle was still in his system.

"You really like Garcelle, don't you?" he asked her.

"I like her a lot."

"I know you do."

"Don't you like her?"

"I do."

"Good."

If only things could be *that* simple.

His eyes fell on the wedding portrait as he stood
and slipped his wallet into his back pocket. His
heart ached, and he knew he needed to be around
his family more than ever.

The Santos house was organized confusion.
Everyone spoke freely in Spanish. Music played.
The television blared. The clang of pots echoed
from the kitchen.

Garcelle wiped the sweat from her brow with her
forearm as she stirred a large pot of seafood stew.
She reached for seasonings and bumped into her
father, who was roasting chickens. "Sorry, Papi," she
said as she bent over slightly to taste the broth.

She felt his eyes on her, and she looked over at

him, with the spoon poised before her lips. When she did turn her head to meet his eyes, she saw the concern he had for her. "I'm okay," she said before he could ask.

"I disagree, Garcelle."

"Did Marisol call?" she asked as she moved to the fridge to remove the bowl of salsa.

"Yes, she did, but don't change the subject, Garcelle." Carlos pierced her with his eyes. "Ever since you and Kade broke up, you have been moping around the house. You hardly eat. You don't play poker anymore. You do nothing but go to school and go to work."

"Papa—"

He held up his hand. "No, let me finish."

Garcelle met her father's eyes.

"If it isn't meant to be, Garcelle, then it just isn't meant to be," he said softly as he reached over to squeeze her hand.

He tugged her hand, and she was wrapped in his loving arms. She didn't want to cry. She *wasn't* going to cry. "I just really thought he was the one, you know? I thought he was for me," she admitted softly.

"I know, *bambina*, I know." Carlos rocked her from side to side like she was still his little girl. "The one for you will come. I promise."

She nodded as she swallowed back any fussy tears. "Perhaps," was all that she said.

"The food ready?" Paco asked as he peeked his head into the kitchen.

"Yes, Son, yes," said Carlos. He patted Garcelle's back comfortingly before he walked over to the kitchen counter and turned up the radio. The sound of Tito Puente filled the air as Carlos extended his hand to Garcelle. She smiled and danced over to him to take his hand, and he spun her.

They used what little room they had to dance around the kitchen as they cooked. Garcelle knew it was her father's way of lightening her mood, and she loved him all the more for it. She loved Kade no less, but the pain she felt about their breakup wasn't quite so sharp anymore.

Hours later, after the seven courses of their holiday dinner were enjoyed, Carlos rose to his feet, with a glass of sangria. He looked around the table, momentarily resting his eyes on each and every person. "I just want to say that I enjoyed spending time with you all. Family is very important to me, and on a day like to day, I am especially thankful to have you all in my life. Never forget the importance, the strength, the support, and the love of family."

Everyone raised their glass in a joyful toast before they sipped from their drinks. Garcelle realized that the fun, good food, family, and friends had kept Kade from her mind for most of the day. She was grateful for that.

One Week Later

Kade knocked on Kahron's office door before he strolled in. He slid his hands into the pockets of his tuxedo pants as he looked down at his brother. "Looking for an escape from all the wedding hoopla?" he asked before folding his tall frame into one of the leather chairs before Kahron's desk.

Kahron shook his head as he leaned back in his chair and wiped his mouth with his hand. "My house has been turned upside, and this is the only spot where I feel like I'm not a visitor in my home."

Kade laughed as he crossed his ankle over his knee. "It will all be over tonight, little brother."

Kahron just mumbled under his breath as he rose and walked over to the bar. He offered Kade a shot of cognac, but he declined.

"Is uh . . . Garcelle coming?" asked Kade.

Kahron watched his brother over the rim of the glass as he sipped his drink. "No."

Kade felt disappointed and relieved.

"Pour me one of those," said a familiar voice.

Kade looked over his shoulder as Kaleb and Kaeden strolled into the office in their tailored tuxedos. Kahron poured the drink and handed it to Kaleb. He laughed as his brother downed it in one gulp and winced afterwards.

"Want another shot?" Kahron asked.

Kaleb scowled. "No," he said in a strangled voice.

Kade looked up, and he saw Kahron's face become transformed. He followed Kahron's line of vision and saw Bianca walk into the room, in a strapless, floor-length, satin dress of the deepest shade of purple.

The men all rose to their feet before they faced her.

"You're a lucky man, brother," Kade drawled.

"Don't I know it," Kahron said as he walked past his brothers to reach his wife.

"So this is where you all are hiding," she said as she raised her face to kiss Kahron briefly before she looked past him. "Now, I must say that this looks like a Sean John ad or something. You are one bunch of sexy . . . ass . . . men."

"Hey," Kade said as if affronted.

She looked up at Kahron. "You're the sexiest of them all, baby."

"I'd like a vote on that," Kade called over to the couple.

"You got that right," Kaleb drawled.

Kaeden straightened his bow tie. "Since Kahron and I look alike, I'll agree with you, Bianca."

She winked at him before she rubbed her hands together. "Okay, the wedding will begin, so I need you all to come out of hiding."

The men headed out of the office just as Bianca turned back around suddenly. "Boys, if you care about me at all, keep your mama and her dang-on J. C. Penneys and Sears catalogs from me today . . . *please.* Deal?"

"Deal," they all said in baritone unison.

Kade knew his mother was in full grandmother mode. She'd been the same way when Reema was pregnant with Kadina. As soon as she knew the egg had been fertilized, she started shopping. Bianca had no clue that the more she showed, the worse his mom was going to get. It would be a full blast of old wives' tales, talk of decorating the nursery, choosing baby names, and everything else baby related under the sun.

Of course, she did it out of nothing but love. It had taken time, but eventually Reema had been glad for the help. Plus, he knew his mother had been looking for a heap load of grandkids from them.

Kade's steps faltered. The way his life was going, there wouldn't be any more kids for him. That thought saddened him. He loved Kadina to death, but he'd always imagined having plenty of children. He frowned deeply.

"What's wrong, Kade?" Kaeden asked as he slapped him soundly on the back. "You look like you're the one headed to the altar."

Kade just shrugged as they walked out the front door and across the lawn to the huge heated tent in the center of the field. The cold bit through his suit, and he sped up his steps. He paused at the entrance to the tent, beside his brothers.

"Wow," Kade said as he shoved his hands inside the pockets of his slacks. "Bianca went all out."

"Yeah," his brothers all said in unison.

The front half of the tent was reserved for the wedding ceremony, and the rear was given over to the cocktail reception and dancing. Big, fat dripping candles were lit in every available spot inside the tent. A multitude of elegantly arranged and deeply colored flowers made the entire tent smell like the inside of a perfume bottle. Thirty people dressed to the nines sat in gold chairs lined up on either side of the aisle. Hank's and Mimi's names floated against the walls in lights as they stood at the altar, before the minister. Kahron, Bianca, and Kadina stood behind them as the best man, maid of honor, and flower girl. The soft strains of Etta James's "At Last" played softly in the background.

I'm late. Garcelle shivered from the cold. Winters in the South were still winters, and she was freezing. The faint wave of heat from inside the tent blew against her body, and she damn near sighed in pleasure. She eased the tent flap back, hoping to slide in and grab a seat in the rear, but she stopped searching when her eyes fell on Kade's profile.

He looked devastatingly gorgeous. His silvery hair contrasted so well with his skin tone and the rich black of his tux. Suddenly, the air outside wasn't quite as cold anymore.

She was late because she had sat for nearly an hour, looking at her dress, which hung on the door, and trying to decide—once and for all—if she was going to attend the wedding. Going to the wedding meant seeing Kade. She was finally in a place where the thought of him didn't hurt as much. Memories of him—his touch, his kisses, his humor, his presence, his love—were easier to recall without regret. The fact that their relationship had ended was less bitter to her.

She was getting over Kade Strong . . . very slowly . . . but very surely.

Garcelle wanted her to attend the wedding, and she had to admit her curiosity about Hank and Mimi's relationship made her want to attend. Besides, she thought it was a good way to prove to herself that she was getting over Kade.

So here she was.

Garcelle forced herself to shift her gaze from Kade. She smiled as she watched Kadina fidget. She looked adorable in her purple satin dress as she played with her basket of flowers and made motions with her matching shoes. Kadina turned and looked over her shoulder. Her eyes widened when they landed on Garcelle. She smiled and waved.

Several people turned to see what had caught Kadina's attention, and Garcelle could have died. Especially when Kade looked over his broad shoulder, and his heated eyes fell on her.

Kade felt the breath literally leave his body as he watched Garcelle step inside the tent and take an empty seat in the rear.

"Wow," Kaleb said in his ear.

Kade knew his rogue of a brother was commenting

on the way Garcelle looked in her short, strapless, fitted sequin dress, which was a deep slate gray, and her matching short fur. Her hair was piled atop her head. Her make-up was dramatic. She looked absolutely stunning. Wow was right.

His heart hammered in his chest as he forced himself to face forward.

The minister's words of love and devotion, coupled with the romantic setting and the sounds of Etta James, made for a beautiful ceremony. It made a woman want to believe in love and a man want to believe in happily ever after.

Several times Garcelle had chanced a look at Kade, only to find his eyes already resting on her. They would both look away.

Garcelle envisioned that it was she who was standing at the altar, in a chic satin gown, with Kade, in his tux, and that they vowed to love one another until the end of time.

But that would never be. *They* would never be.

Coming here was a mistake.

Etta's singing of love at last grew louder, until her voice echoed inside the tent. Hank bent down to kiss his bride, and Garcelle rose from her seat and fled from the tent and the visions of a life she would never have.

19

One Week Later

Kade squatted down by the three-foot marble headstone of his wife. He used his hand to brush away the few leaves covering her grave.

"I miss you a lot, you know," he said, shifting to sit on the ground. "I guess you do know that. You probably can see everything going on down here." He licked his lips as the winds picked up. "So I guess you probably know about Garcelle."

He smiled at the thought of Garcelle. "You would like her. She's funny and smart and full of life, and . . . and . . . she made . . . *makes* me happy, Reema," he admitted. "But I guess you probably know that, too," he said, with a laugh.

"She's so good with Kadina, and she talks about you all the time with her, and she would help me raise Kadina to be just the type of woman you would want her to be."

He looked around as the limbs of the trees swayed from side to side.

Seeing Garcelle at the wedding last week had

brought it home that she, too, meant a lot to him. When he looked up after the wedding ceremony to find she was gone, he knew that the ceremony had touched her as well. He knew that she loved him still.

I'm here living and breathing and loving you, but I'm not about to fight with a ghost. . . .

"I don't want you to think that I will ever forget you or stop loving you . . . because I won't, but I love Garcelle," he admitted, blinking away tears as he cleared his throat. "I *really* love her, and I just don't want you to think that my loving her takes away from anything we shared together."

The winds whipped around him, and he felt comforted.

"Reema, it's time for me to move on, and I know now that you would want that for me." He rose to his feet with ease and brushed the dirt from his pants. "I will never forget you. I promise you that."

"Good night, Donnie," Garcelle called out to the gruff owner as she walked out the front door of the restaurant. She pulled her print sweater cap on before she searched in her purse for her keys.

"Garcelle."

She looked up. Kade stood there, leaning against his car and holding a large bouquet of roses. His usual Dickies uniform was gone, replaced by a black suit and an open black shirt, worn under a crisp tailored wool coat that made him devastatingly handsome. She felt surprised, pleased, and confused by his presence. "Hello, Kade," she said, feeling awkward in his presence. It had been a week since the wedding. She had just gotten her equilibrium back, and here he was, throwing her off again.

He pushed off the vehicle and walked over to her. The cold wind blew around them, and the scent of his cologne reached her as he held the bouquet out to her. "For you."

Garcelle bit her bottom lip as she accepted it. Their hands touched briefly, and there was still nothing but sparks. "What's going on? What's this all about?"

He reached up and lightly touched her chin. "It's about me being happy, and you make me happy. The last two months have been hell, but I'm ready for my own little slice of heaven in your arms . . . in your life."

Garcelle closed her eyes and released a long stream of air through pursed lips as she fought for composure.

Kade continued. "You were right. I wasn't ready before. I wasn't able to fully accept you being in my life. All I knew then was that I loved you, and I wanted you in my life. It took time for me to realize that I *need* you."

Garcelle buried her face in the bouquet as she got her thoughts and her words together. "You really hurt me, Kade," she admitted. "I gave you distance. I didn't push. I didn't do a Zorrie on you—"

"I know. I know. Can I show you something?" he asked as he reached for her hand.

Her reluctance was obvious. "Kade, I don't know. . . ."

"Please."

"Why are you doing this to me?" Garcelle looked into his eyes.

Kade stepped closer to her and brought one hand up to caress the side of her face and then her nape. "Do you love me?"

"My life is fine. Why not let it be, Kade?"

"Do . . . you . . . love . . . me?"

Garcelle let her head fall back as he continued to massage her neck. "Kade . . ."

He used his hand to turn her head so that their eyes locked. "Do you love me?" he whispered, his cool breath fanning her lips.

"Yes," she admitted in a heated rush. "Yes, I love you."

"Come on," he said, reaching for her hand and lightly pulling her toward the SUV.

They rode in silence. Their hands were entwined atop the console in between their seats.

"Where are we going?" she asked, still trying to decide if she was happy or not being with the man she loved. The same man who had hurt her.

"Home," he said simply.

Garcelle said nothing else. "Your home or my home?" she asked.

He didn't answer her until they turned down the road leading to his house. It appeared every room in the house was lit up. She had to admit it was a warm and inviting sight.

"If you think bringing me here to prove you can have sex in your wife's house—"

"Our home," he told her as he shut the vehicle off.

"Huh?"

"You asked if I was taking you to your home or mine, and I am saying this is *our* home."

He climbed out of the vehicle and left her sitting there, more confused than ever. "Our home?" she asked as she watched him jog up the stairs and into the house.

Garcelle dropped her roses on the driver's seat as she scrambled out of the vehicle and up the stairs and into the house. As soon as she crossed the threshold, she gasped in surprise.

There was a trail of rose petals and candles in tall vases leading down the hall and into the den. "Kade," she called out.

"I want you to walk around the whole house first and then meet me in the den," he called back to her.

"What?"

"Just do it."

And she did. Room by room after room. Upstairs and downstairs. And each room she found completely devoid of furniture. No throw rugs. No curtains. No towels in the bathrooms. No beds in the bedrooms. Nothing. There was absolutely no furniture. The house looked like it had just been purchased and was waiting for someone to turn it into a home.

What was going on?

In Kade's bedroom, she found the same emptiness, but what really shocked her was that the large wedding photo was gone from its spot on the wall. She left the room and went racing down the stairs. Once in the front hall, she followed the beautifully lit path into the den. "I'm coming, Kade," she called out.

"Come on," he urged.

In the center of the room, Kade was down on one knee, surrounded by a thick bed of rose petals. He held a ring box in his outstretched hand.

"Kade?"

"Come to me."

Garcelle hated to walk across the petals, but she wanted to be close to him. She tiptoed until she stood before him, with her eyes locked on his. "Kade, this so beautiful," she sighed, her accent very heavy.

"Garcelle, I am more than ready to welcome you into my life, my home, and my heart. I want this to be our home so that we can share our lives together and make our own memories. Our own babies. Our own history. We'll start fresh. We'll decorate it together. We'll make it ours." He took a deep breath and smiled up at her. "Will you marry me, Garcelle?"

She was touched beyond words. Her heart overflowed with love for him. She couldn't begin to explain how much *all of it* meant to her.

"Yes. Yes. Yes. I'll marry you. I will marry you, Kade Strong," she said, with a soft, teasing tone, as she bent down to kiss him firmly on the lips.

As he slid the three-carat solitaire onto her finger, Garcelle fell to her knees before him. She grasped his face, and they shared a dozen or more kisses before he pressed her body down upon the plush bed of rose petals.

They undressed one another slowly, as if to cherish every moment of their union. They sighed in pleasure at the feel of each other's naked flesh. His hard frame pressed against her soft curves as they explored each other's bodies. Sweat made many of the rose petals cling to their bodies as they rolled about and kissed and whispered words of nothing but love and devotion for one another. And when he filled her with his hardness, each stroke united them at a far deeper level than the physical one. It was the merging of two souls destined to become one.

Epilogue

Six Months Later

"It's a boy! It's a boy!"

Almost everyone in the entire waiting room of the labor and delivery wing of Colleton Medical Center jumped to their feet and rushed Kahron, with congratulations.

Garcelle turned to hug Kade tightly, with excitement, as she took in the rest of the family.

"Hot damn, the Strong name lives on!" Kael Strong roared, with a pump of his fist in the air. He pulled Lisha to him and twirled her around the waiting room.

"Yes, but it was a King that brought him into the world," Hank countered as he lifted his wife high in his arms. "Ain't that right, Mimi?"

"You are *always* right, Big Daddy," Mimi purred in her real voice as she rubbed his big belly. He giggled like the Pillsbury Doughboy.

Carlos stepped up to shake Kahron's hand. "Congratulations, Kahron."

"Thank you, Carlos. Thank you." Kahron's face beamed.

Once Kade asked Carlos for his daughter's hand in marriage, the Strongs and the Kings had pulled the Santos clan right into their midst.

"Pay up, you two. Y'all lost," Kaleb boasted to Kaitlyn and Kaeden, with his hand outstretched.

Kaitlyn reached in her purse and roughly pushed the fifty-dollar bill into Kaleb's hand. "I thought they said if she carried low, it was a girl," she grumbled good-naturedly.

"See if I listen to you and those old wives' tales again," Kaeden told Kaityln as he counted out fifty dollars from his wallet and handed the bills to his brother.

Kadina left her spot in between Garcelle and Kade and cleared her throat as she looked up at her Uncle Kaleb. "Remember, you forgot my birthday money because you didn't have any cash on you, Uncle Kaleb," she said as she eyed the wad in his hand, with a toothy smile.

Garcelle, Kadina, and everyone in the room laughed as Kaleb peeled off two ten-dollar bills to give her. Kadina cleared her throat again, and Kaleb peeled off a twenty.

"Happy birthday. We straight?" Kaleb asked as he mussed Kadina's bangs.

"All the time. All the time," Kadina said as she counted her money and walked back to her father and future stepmother.

She handed the money to Garcelle. "We'll put it in your piggy bank when we get home," Garcelle promised her.

"When can we see my little girl?" Hank asked as Mimi rubbed his lower back.

"Right now. But try and keep it down, okay?" said Kahron. He opened the door and held it open as everyone filed out.

Kade grabbed Garcelle around the waist from behind. "You sure you want to be a part of this circus?" he asked.

"There's nothing more I want in the world," she told him before she turned, wrapped her arms around his neck, and kissed him deeply, with lots and lots of love, passion, and chemistry, which burned hot like fire.

Dear Readers,

I hoped you felt the love, passion, and fire between Kade and Garcelle. Theirs was truly a love that was able to overcome *all* obstacles.

This joint Strong Family / Hot Holtsville Series is becoming near and dear to me. I am truly enjoying each and every one of these couples as they fall headfirst in love. *Fever* is coming soon. It is book three in the Strong Family Series and book five in the Hot Holtsville Series. In *Fever* you will see just how Kaeden Strong finally finds the courage to go after the sexy Jade Prince. It will be a sexy, funny, and endearing book, which I hope you all will enjoy.

Also, don't forget that *Show and Tell*, the sequel to my critically acclaimed mainstream debut, *Live and Learn*, is on its way to you all in March 2008. Catch up with Dom, Alize, Cristal, and Moët. You won't believe how the lessons they learned go right out the window as they each face more drama than ever.

Thanks again to all of you for your loyal support. I appreciate and cherish you all.

As always, Love 2 Live & Live 2 Love.
Best,
Niobia♥